RAVE REVIEWS FOR THE WORK OF DOUGLAS CLEGG!

"Every bit as good as the best works of Stephen King, Peter Straub, or Dan Simmons. What is most remarkable is not how well Clegg provides chills, but how quickly he is able to do so."

—*Hellnotes*

"Clegg's imagery is intense, horrific, but he paints with a poet's hand. Horror at its finest."

—*Publishers Weekly* (Starred Review)

"Unforgettable!"

—*The Washington Post*

"Doug Clegg is one of horror's most captivating voices."

—*BookLovers*

"Clegg possesses a master's unsparing touch for horror. [*You Come When I Call You* is] a brilliant achievement of occult fiction."

—*Rue Morgue*

"Douglas Clegg's short stories can chill the spine so effectively that the reader should keep paramedics on standby!"

—Dean Koontz

"*You Come When I Call You* is the first major literary event in the genre for the year. I've never had a work of fiction affect me more deeply. This is an absolute must read!"

—Garrett Peck, *Hellnotes*

"Douglas Clegg's writing is like a potent drink that goes down with deceptive smooth̶n̶e̶s̶s̶ ... knocks you on your de̶r̶..."

—̶ ...*ronline*

DOWN IN THE CRYPT

The steps down were worn and slippery; damp scum of some kind covered them. Jim took them slowly, one at a time, until he reached the fifth step down, and then he was in the crypt.

He shone the flashlight around—various names were on the graves, and two table graves rose at the center of the marble floor.

Jim made sure that no one was lurking at any corner of the crypt. Then he went to the great slabs that lay on top of the two graves at the middle of the small, square room. He shined the light upon one.

It read:

Genevieve Campion Gravesend. Died at her beloved Balmoral Cottage, Fenwick, Connecticut, during the year of our Lord 1891.

A bas relief rose at the foot of the crypt of a curious but beautiful angel, with wings that seemed to come from its scalp and sweep along its shoulders.

Jim turned the light on the other grave. It was perfectly smooth alabaster. He touched the stone, and felt its ice. There was no name, no image, nothing upon it. He set the flashlight on Genevieve's crypt, its light aimed for the edge of the other's lid.

It was the doorway to Death, and he had to open it.

He pressed his fingers beneath the slab, but it didn't budge. His wrist ached from the effort.

He lifted the flashlight again, and directed the beam to the walls. There were a few markers on the wall, but someone had written across the wall in what might've been blood:

WAIT FOR WHAT WILL COME.

MISCHIEF

DOUGLAS
CLEGG

LEISURE BOOKS NEW YORK CITY

A LEISURE BOOK®

September 2000

Published by

Dorchester Publishing Co., Inc.
276 Fifth Avenue
New York, NY 10001

ISBN 0-8439-4766-7

For Don D'Auria

Thanks to the team at Hearst, led by Jennifer Marek, for the wonderful stuff. Special thank yous to Kate with a Z., Andrew LeCount, Maria Liu, and the whole .com gang. As always, thank you to Rich Chizmar and Cemetery Dance Publications, and Dorchester Publishing. Special thanks to Tommy Dreiling. Above all, this one could not have been written without Raul Silva.

Be sure to check out Douglas Clegg's website at:
http://www.douglasclegg.com or e-mail
Doug at dclegg@douglasclegg.com

MISCHIEF

Do what thou wilt shall be the whole of the law.

In one sense a poet, however sublime, is limited by his mental power and capacity, and by the circumstances of the molecular changes in the brain. . . . Let me explain in a few words how the question of Magick may be defined as the practical ability to set in right motion the necessary forces. . . .

—Aleister Crowley

Once upon a time there was a boy named Jack who lived with his poor mother. All they had left was one cow, and one day Jack went to market with the cow to sell it so he and his mother could eat. But on the way, he met an old woman who offered him three magic beans in exchange for the cow. "These will bring great fortune to whoever plants them in his garden."

"How will something so small bring fortune, crone?" Jack asked.

"There is a place," the woman said, "that is beyond the world, but to reach it, one must take chances. What do you want more than anything in the world, boy?"

Jack thought for a minute and then told her.

—from a retelling of the classic fairy tale,
"Jack and the Beanstalk"

Prologue

"What do you want more than anything else in the world?"

"You know. I already told you."

"Say it."

"You can't bring back the dead."

"There's a way to do it."

"It's a game," he said, mostly to himself. "It's only a game, right? Like a room in my mind. It *is* a game."

"If you say so. Believe what you want. No one ever said you couldn't."

"It has to be," he said. "It's some kind of game. A test. Part of the initiation."

The wind brushed through his hair as he stood at the open window, looking down.

It was a hell of a long drop. He stood on the ledge at the top of the tower. He imagined dropping a water balloon and counting till ten before it hit the pavement. That's what it would be like. He'd drop and then it would all be over.

"Every game has its rules. I just need to know what the rules of this one are," he said, hoping the other boy would tell him something—anything—that would give away this game.

He kept feeling the tug of the earth—not gravity, but the need to be there, the need to leave the tower and return to the ground again. He couldn't keep from looking down.

The more he looked at the distance between where he stood and the earth below, the more interesting it became. It didn't seem like a fall, it seemed like he could just step over into it, as if . . . his eyes were playing tricks on him . . . but it was as if it weren't a long way down at all.

The other boy stood behind him and whispered, "It's just like a corridor, isn't it? You look down and see the drive and the stones and the fountain, but it changes when you watch it, the edge of your vision wraps around it; and it becomes a long corridor and it makes you feel as if you could just step out into it, and walk that long way to its end, to find out what waits there for you. You can't go back because you know what waits for you there. You can't stay where you are. You must go forward."

"What's there?" he asked.

"What you want. More than anything."

"No," he said.

"Go on. You'll see. You can't stay on the ledge, can you? You can't go back. You know what's there. You can only go on. You want to, I can tell."

"What's there?" he repeated.

But the boy behind him didn't answer. He may have stepped away.

"It has to be a game," he said. "This can't be real. This can't be."

He stood alone at the top of the tower.

And then, he stepped off the ledge.

PART ONE
CRIME

"Not far from this village, perhaps about two miles, there is a little valley, or rather lap of land, among high hills, which is one of the quietest places in the whole world. . . ."

—Washington Irving,
The Legend of Sleepy Hollow

Jack said to his mother, "Don't worry. I'm going to go out into the world and seek my fortune, and then I will return with gold aplenty." His mother told him, "Jack, whatever you do, do not climb that beanstalk. There can't be anything good up there and there are sure to be monsters in places unknown. Bad enough that you

17

bought those beans with our last cow. Bad enough you have a dream at all. Bad enough that you have wasted your life dreaming. You would be a fool to go up that beanstalk."

But that is, in fact, just what Jack did.

Chapter One
Harrow

1

All houses, at one time or another, hold both life and death. One assumes that land, also, will have absorbed the life of the dying, and will bring forth, in spring, the bird and the deer and the fox from her womb despite the small tragedies that continue each day.

Imagine a moment in prehistory, a falling mastodon preyed upon by hunters, or further back, a large reptilian ancestor of the hawk as it takes down some small creature, or even the brontosaur dying at the edge of some primordial swamp; can there be evil in such an environment? Without human life, was there the

Douglas Clegg

sense among what lived then that a place could be singularly bad?

Imagine next the upheaval of earth and sea, the great land masses in motion, the eons passing as what is now North America formed, as vegetation covered its Northeast area, and as a river cut through a section known today as the Hudson Valley. Where is the dividing line between a place of darkness and a place of light? Is it all the creation of the human imagination, which notices that curious slant of light over the sloping hill, the jagged and lonesome tor thrust above the river? Is it merely perception that provides the sense—the vibration, if you will—that this spot carries with it a sense of unremitting dread?

Once, the property in question was thick with forest, bounteous with game and birdsong, and stank of that fertility known to the virgin wilderness. Then, at some point in the earth's history, human life touched this place, perhaps blood was spilled in some fight, or perhaps a ritual of belief was enacted.

Perhaps nothing of significance took place here, at Harrow, at the edge of Watch Point.

All one can suppose is that something triggered the birth of a dark spot upon this particular parcel of land. Perhaps the great tombs of the pharaohs of Egypt, or the pyramids of the Sun and Moon in ancient Tenochtitlán, or the monolithic heads along Easter Island, or the

TRY NAWH TEA FLANN

waters at Lourdes, or the Delphic Oracle with its earth-cracks and smoke, had also been consecrated by something deep, rich, and eternal—and perhaps for every good and sacred place as these that the human race discovers, there is an equal number of what could, for lack of a better term, be considered bad places.

Blind spots. Tainted lands.

There have been reports: a town in Virginia nearly destroyed by some form of supernature; a place in the desert of the Southwest, perhaps vaporized by wind and fire, perhaps taken over by something more sinister; a colony in what is now called North Carolina, in which the entire population vanished in a short period of time, without a trace; a New England borough smashed as if, according to one witness, "by the fist of a giant child." There are other such places throughout the world—but to America, and to one particular corner of America, our attention must now turn.

The land that came to be known by the English as Camden's Hundred, and then later, Harrow, had a magnetic feel to it that both attracted and repelled. In early accounts, it was described as uninhabitable, and the soil too rocky to plant, the woods too dense to clear. The natives of the area had no interest in it as territory; neither did the Dutch.

It was known as an unclean place as far back as the late 1600s, when the Dutch settlements had grown along the banks and slopes that rose above the river. There were rumors of vile creatures living in the woods, and wild hounds howling on Candlemas Eve and All Hallows'. Later, as New York became a state, there was a story that an old Hessian soldier haunted the woods, and another that a woman dressed completely in white walked along what could only be called the mist-enshrouded hills of Watch Point beneath a full moon.

Yet, for all that, it was one of the most beautiful landscapes along the Hudson Valley, and it was no surprise to anyone when, after the Civil War, the great robber baron, Justin Gravesend, rich from war, cattle, and railroads, purchased seventy-five acres for his own purposes just outside the village.

What *was* surprising was what he did with the land.

2

The house stood through years of neglect; the legends of its power waned; only the elderly could recall the story of its early history; it fell into ruins; and then, it began to reform, and grow, spreading over the beautiful valley with new life.

No one noticed the growth, the towers resurrecting under the loving care of architects and builders; the new additions grafted onto the old halls; the parapets smoothed over with cement and brick; the old glass replaced with new, the fallen stones wedged back into their places; the vines and brambles hacked away with blade and mower.

But can a house live?

A boy named Jim Hook would never have thought so, when, years later, he found himself confronted with the place called Harrow.

Chapter Two
Jim's Early Life

1

When Jim Hook was four, his brother saved him from drowning, even though no one ever knew it but the two of them.

They'd been playing in a neighbor's swimming pool when no one was around to watch, and Stephen was doing stunt dives from the board, making his little brother laugh whenever he did a belly flop.

Jim tried to imitate one such dive from the shallow end of the pool, but when he went down he was too close to the edge and hit his head. Confused for a moment, and feeling the owie on his scalp, he went down into the water, unsure of which way was up, and he was no longer in the shallow end.

He was a terrible dog-paddler, and he felt himself sinking down, and felt something dark clutch at him in the silky blue water—something with a face, although it was like a mask.

And then his brother pulled him up and hugged him tight and told Jim not to scare him like that. They were closer after that, and Jim never forgot his brother's lifting him out of the water, and the way his brother practically wept for joy when he saw Jim breathing again, spitting water all over the place.

"How do you know you're my brother?"

"I look like you."

"How you gonna make your big bro proud?"

"By doing the best I can," Jim said at four, then at six, and again at eight, and then at nine, and sometimes, in his dreams, he said it again.

His older brother's favorite singer was some old guy Jim never heard on the radio, named Cat Stevens, so Cat Stevens became Jim's favorite singer, too, and he knew the words to songs like "Tea for the Tillerman" and "Oh Very Young," even when other kids in school looked at him strangely when they saw his collection of CDs; and his brother liked playing basketball, so Jim had begun to love basketball, and when his brother took up cross-country, Jim took up running as well so he could run behind his brother when he was home for holidays and all summer long. His brother slapped on Old Spice some mornings, and then would offer Jim the little white bottle to try out, too. "It's not the best, Squirt," Stephen would say, slapping the stuff around Jim's neck, "but the girls seem to like it fine."

"Yeah!" Jim would say.

When Stephen began dating, Jim would try to tag along for as much of the afternoon or evening as he could, and sometimes Stephen would even let him ride along in the backseat when he took one of his many girlfriends out to the movies, as long as the movie was PG. Some of the girls told him how cute he was, and then told Stephen he was even cuter for dragging his baby brother with him. And Jim would sit in the dark movie theater, and not even care what the movie was, because Stephen would sit next to him and let him hold the big popcorn and the gigantic cup of Coke and didn't even act embarrassed when other friends of his from school ran into him with his girlfriend and little brother out on a date.

It was like that with the two of them. Jim was "Squirt," and Stephen was "Big Bro," which sometimes became "Big Bear," and if you had ever told Jim that his brother might one day never come home again, he would've sworn you were the biggest and meanest liar on the face of the whole earth.

Douglas Clegg

2

When Jim was only eleven, something unusual happened to him.

This was back when he lived in what he later came to think of as the Big House on the Hill in a town called Bronxville just outside New York City. Contrary to its name—with associations with the Bronx in the city—Bronxville was a one-square-mile showplace village of beautiful houses and perfectly manicured lawns.

Jim's family was not considered wealthy in Bronxville, and the house, despite Jim's later memories of it, was not, in fact, big.

But to that little boy, it was a mansion of many rooms, and he had grown up in the house knowing his father and mother would always make sure the heat was turned up to keep him warm in the winter, and there would always be someone to take care of him when he was lonely or scared. His world up to that point had consisted of nannies and eavesdropping on his parents and their friends having drinks in the living room and talking about things that seemed sophisticated to him; and of course, his brother, Stephen, the one he looked up to the most.

Stephen was a junior in a far away high school, the one their dad had gone to, and came home during the winter holidays—Jim felt—to spend as much time with his little brother as possible.

And the something unusual that happened to Jim happened during one of those bleak winter nights.

3

Stephen came to him, in his room, dressed in his usual khakis and starchy cotton shirt, a striped blue and white tie failing in its knot at his collar. His prep school look. He had his big green down jacket in his arms like a baby. A dusting of snow clung to his hair and melted off the lime-green rubber of his Eddie Bauer duck-shoes.

Jim sat up in bed, setting down the comic book he'd been reading way past his bedtime, and said hi to his older brother. The clock was ticking too loudly—Stephen had given the alarm clock to him for Christmas the previous week, but if Jim wound it too tight, which he did, the ticking was almost like someone walking rapidly up an echoing staircase.

Jim glanced at the clock.

It was nearly one in the morning.

He looked back at his older brother. Stephen offered that lopsided smile that he usually reserved for occasions of goofy misfortune, like when Jim had forgotten and had left the sprinklers running too long, turning the lawn to mush, or the time that Stephen had gotten kissed by a girl years before and had run to tell Jim that it was his first kiss ever.

Stephen said, "Jimbo, don't let the bastards get you down," and Jim gave a raspberry in reply because their father had just been getting after Stephen to tone down his language in front of his younger brother.

"That's a bad word," Jim giggled.

"How'd you know you're my brother?" Stephen asked, laughing.

"I'm too old and sleepy for this."

"Old man that you are," Stephen laughed. "Come on."

"Okay. 'Cause I look like you."

"And how you gonna make your big bro proud?"

"By doing the best I can," Jim said sleepily, pulling the covers up around his neck. "Now let me go to sleep."

"That's all," Stephen said. "Oh, and whatever you do, just remember, every secret was meant to be told and every door was meant to be opened."

"Okay," Jim said, sleepily, wondering why Stephen was home so soon when it was snowing so bad.

Stephen and his dad were driving back from the city, but the weather reports were bad, and his mom had asked them to just stay at Gramma's in Greenwich Village for another night till the snow was through.

Mischief

Jim loved the snow.

Stephen left the room they shared, switching off the light. He said, "Get some shut-eye, Squirt. "Mom'll probably need you tomorrow for all kinds of stuff. Wait for what'll come."

Jim dropped his comic book to the carpet and closed his eyes. In his dreams, he saw a big snake eating its own tail, and for some reason this didn't scare him or bother him. He felt a kind of peace from the dream, but something startled him from his sleep.

There was some noise in the house, and Jim wasn't even sure if he was dreaming or not. He got out of bed, tossing the covers nearly to the floor. He went in the direction of the sound, which was coming from upstairs.

Sometimes, in winter, the wind would blow so hard that it would start things creaking in the house. Jim went up the stairs, and followed the sound—

Now it was just a scratching.

Words formed in his mind.

Words of panic:

Something's coming through.

He stood at the foot of the wooden steps up to the small attic door.

Something was scratching at the other side of the door. Jim, never fond of the attic, took a few hesitant tiptoes up.

The scratching became wild. Something was sniffing on the other side of the attic door.

Douglas Clegg

A wild animal.

Then, for a second, it sounded like someone was throwing furniture around the attic while a wild animal scratched in desperation at the door.

Something's coming through.

A voice whispered, "Be he alive or be he dead."

Or he had imagined someone said it.

Slowly, his heart pounding in his chest, he took one step after another backward, and when he was in the hall, his feet on the carpet, he turned and ran back downstairs to his bedroom, diving under the sheets, not bothering to pick his comforter back up from the floor. He squeezed his eyelids shut, and tried to ignore the pee that had soaked his pajamas. He didn't want to be in a world of fear. And this had made him very afraid. He wanted to be in a room by himself. People spoke softly from the other side of the door in the room—it was a room in his head, and he was locked in, all safe, and there was a little window to look out of, but his fear was beyond the window. He was safe inside. The room seemed real. It was the beginning of a dream. He fell asleep again, after a long while.

When Jim awoke the next morning, Stephen's bed remained untouched.

It was only later, when he found his mom crying in her bathrobe, the telephone dropped to the floor, its coiling cord unwinding slowly, that

Jim knew something unusual had happened.

His dad and brother had died in a wreck out on the icy highway the night before. The Jeep had flipped, and then a Lonsdale Farms milk truck had rammed into them as both Stephen and his father hung upside down in the car, held in by their shoulder harnesses and seat belts. His brother had stopped breathing at precisely the moment that Jim had watched him enter the bedroom to give his last words of advice.

All Jim remembered, later, was that he cried his eyes out. That's what he thought of it: that his eyes had literally been wept out of him, that they had melted down into the carpet and floorboards and he had no tears left in him ever again for anyone.

Jim had talked himself out of this memory by the time he was a teenager. For how could he have seen his brother in his room at the very moment his brother had gone to heaven?

4

Then, a few years later, Jim entered the same prep school his father and Stephen had both attended. The night of the visitation was long forgotten, as all children forget their brief moments with the unknowable as they learn what they are meant to believe, just as the dream of the snake had evaporated from his memory.

Douglas Clegg

By that time, Jim and his mother had had to move to a town called Yonkers, and lived in a one-bedroom apartment together; Jim slept on the sofa most nights without unfolding it.

He had watched his father's family and his mother fight, even at Stephen and his father's funeral; he had watched his mother and the bankers fight; and he had watched his mother fight with almost anyone who came to the door. Sometimes, when the fights got awful, Jim would go into the bathroom and play his CDs—with the headphones on—but sometimes, he just closed his eyes and imagined that instead of shouts and curses, he heard furniture being thrown, glass breaking.

Once, the medicine chest mirror broke, and he couldn't remember ever having taken his fist and smashed it.

After a few years of fighting, his mom had no spark left within her except seething resentment for Jim's uncles and aunts and Gramma.

His mother told Jim that it was his father's dream to see one of his sons graduate from Harrow, so calls were made, rigorous academic tests were taken, scholarships and loans were applied for, and eventually—after receiving no funds from the school for seventh and eighth grade, Jim managed to get in to the prep school for his freshman year in high school.

How you gonna make your big bro proud?

When Jim was at school, he forgot the world

that his mother now occupied: she worked at a branch of the very same bank that had taken away the Big House on the Hill; she even accepted the small checks from Gramma to make sure Jim had the right clothes and pocket money for school. But that was as far as his mother's pride would go.

Now it was up to him.

Jim met a girl named Lark and by sophomore year was going steady; he didn't excel at cross-country, but enjoyed it as one of the few sports in which he could compete; and he wanted more than anything to graduate from Harrow, the school his brother had gone to, the school his father had also attended.

He knew that if he just hung in for the whole four-year stretch, he would, as his dead brother had advised, not let the bastards get him down.

And that's when things really began to happen.

Chapter Three
The School

1

From the Harrow Academy Brochure:

Harrow Academy is a college preparatory school located amid the beauty of the Hudson Valley that educates boys from seventh through twelfth grade. To help our students succeed in a complex and changing world, we seek to inspire a passion for learning, an enthusiasm for athletic endeavor, a striving for excellence, a celebration of diversity, and a commitment to service. The well-rounded man of letters and skill is our goal. Families sometimes resist the single-sex experience for their sons, but our graduates have found that the sense of brotherhood and competition toward excellence fostered within these walls, as well as the traditional boy's school experience, are well worth the separation from the outside world.

On graduating from Harrow, students are fully prepared for a demanding, rigorous university program; but it is our hope that knowledge acquired here leads to a wisdom that will serve the individual, the school, and the world. Harrow is not the end of our students' education, but the beginning of our leading them from childhood into manhood.

We will make men of your sons.

The rest is up to them.

Thus, our motto:

Journey with Us into Enlightenment, and Wait for What Will Come.

2

The school was there, waiting for him.

3

Jim adapted to prep school life more easily than many others, and because his goal remained in his head—that he must get through it, that he must push out to the other side of Harrow come hell or high water, that he must make his mother proud and get the best education he could so he could one day make the kind of money to help his mother out and show his grandmother that they were worth something after all—that goal remained with him.

But as with all people burning to get something from some dire situation, Jim Hook got sidetracked at times. He wasn't the best or the worst student. He wasn't confident in his abilities. He didn't feel terribly coordinated.

And then, of course, the school could, itself, be intimidating.

4

Architecturally, Harrow was a property that resembled a shambles more than a unified structure. It gathered up a hill and a cliff around it, like a skirt around hips. Three towers rose from its front—and from behind, the great arches of what had once been an abbey.

It defined the town of Watch Point, which existed beneath its stone and iron gaze like a disobedient, slovenly child.

No one could miss the turrets and the bell tower, no matter where one walked in the village. Few in the village commented on the Harrow Academy, and even fewer went to visit the campus, except for the basic deliveries. It was as if an invisible line had been drawn in a crooked oval around the sprawling property. Certainly, the students and faculty didn't mingle well with the villagers, who lived a very different life of daily struggle. Harrow was the youthful Ivory Tower looking out over the river and village, and it was as different a world from Watch Point as could exist.

At the foot of the drive up to Harrow, a wall and gate rose up to mark off the school from the outer world.

The gate was often strung with vines, which were cut back every spring and which died in the fall; thistle and crown sculpture sprouted along the wrought iron of the gate spears. The gate was never locked, except in summer, when one had to park outside the wall and walk through the unattended guard booth.

A false guard booth made of stone waited at either side of the gate—three-foot-high carvings of griffins and unicorns, cracked and pockmarked with age and abuse. Hiding the old brick of the Great Wall of Harrow, the pricker vines and ivy grew and spread, while a sprinkling of bent and scraggly trees stretched along the periphery.

Security was lax at Harrow for several reasons. First, there had never been more than a half dozen incidents of note between the villagers and the school in the past twenty years. One teacher in the 1980s had conducted an affair

Mischief

with a local minister's wife, which caused no
end of scandal for a school that had a minor
affiliation with the Episcopal Church. Six members of the soccer team had been expelled in
1994 for stealing shoes from McCary's Shoe
Shinery out by the highway—but in retaliation,
the two McCary boys broke into the library and
ransacked it. Then, there was the case of a student who set fire to Gravesend Chapel up on
Bald Hill, several years back, and then a student
had died and it was just one of those emotional
and terrible things that happens once in a great
while with adolescents.

But in general, security was not an issue. Harrow had a strict honor code; outsiders rarely
came through Watch Point; and Watch Pointers
tended to just keep away from the school.

Driving up to the school would've been im-
pressive, had the overgrowth from the Cedars
of Lebanon not blocked so much of the view—
and what wasn't tree was shrub, as boxwoods
had been imported to the campus in the early
1970s. The trees and hedges had been gifts from
various alumni who had actually gone on to
great inheritance and fame—and yearly, more
were added, as if this were the only gift former
students could imagine for their alma mater.
The brush had taken over the edges of paths
and the narrow avenues like an encroaching
jungle.

41

Then, the sun broke through the under-growth and overhanging branches. There she was.

Harrow.

Much has been written over the years of its mesh of styles and posturings—the Roman-esque, the Gothic, the Georgian, the Medieval, the Modern, the Eastlake arches and Victorian flourishes on the West Wing, and the nearly Spanish-Moroccan rococo intricacies of the East, all of it thrown together, creating an effect that ended up being pleasing to the eye but nonetheless disturbing in its essential disso-nance. The old statue of St. George and the Dragon, at the center of the fountain around which the circular drive bled, still guarded the steps up to the school as it had since before the school's creation, when Harrow was simply a house.

Around the sides of the house were paths and walks and ways too narrow to be called roads and too wide to be properly termed paths. They went around and between buildings. If you walked too far up the middle path, nearly a mile, you'd come to what the boys called Ha-drian's Wall; it overlooked the Hudson River. The school itself was three distinct buildings. From a distance, it was more than an estate.

It was a citadel.

5

The boys school called Harrow didn't stand a chance, because there was too much about it that made it the wrong place—no, more than that, the most dreadful place.

Called the 'Row by generations of boys since its founding as a school in the 1940s, it was an abnormally large mansion situated picturesquely on the Hudson River Valley. It was marble and brick and every stone and material that could possibly be a bit too much—that was the 'Row.

Its first headmaster, a middle-aged man named Chambers, still haunted its corridors at the age of eighty, occasionally snapping at one of the younger boys whose tie was askew. He was the terror of the middle school wing (known as East), but the older boys (who attended classes in West) tended to treat him as their addled old grandfather.

The school was once quite beautiful, but owing to its rapid growth—the mansion it had once been was smallish for a growing school—an additional, and cheaply made wing had been added. It was dull and brick and square, and was perhaps a fitting tribute to the architecture of 1970—it housed the gym and rooms for some of the boys who boarded, while the rest of the "tribe," as old Chambers himself called the Harrow boys, went home to their families down in the city or nearby daily.

The cafeteria—called the Grampion Memorial Dining Hall—was nearly elegant, with chandeliers and blessings over mashed potatoes; the chairs in the classrooms were torturous; half of the instructors were fresh out of college, and the other half had been working the Harrow system since at least the 1980s, a few a bit longer when they, too, had been fresh out of college.

The school was neither the best nor the worst—it was a solidly mediocre addition to the roster of private schools for boys, and although the occasional novelist or actor or financial wizard or presidential adviser had happened to have been born full-grown from its many passages, it was equally true that at least a half dozen corporate thieves and half-assed nothings had also emerged from its less-than-hallowed entryway.

Fourteen different classrooms were in its upper floors, twelve offices on its main floor, plus a large lounge leading to the inner entrance to the rather inadequate library, which had once been something of a conservatory, and several storage areas. There was a Romanesque look to the main house—gothic arches, with Eastlake touches—and yet the most incongruous additions and touches were added long after the original creator had passed away.

The final effect, the villagers often commented, was that Harrow had the look of a military academy or—some joked—a convent, although it was neither.

The building materials were a mix of brick and granite, brownstone and rough-hewn fieldstone; and yet, Harrow had the feel of being one piece, as if its shambling form were meant to come together under some unknown artisan's eye.

Courtyards grew between the stretch of buildings; the triple towers of the house seemed like anchors holding all the pieces together; and the property—forty-five acres total, although only a quarter of this was usable for the school, as the rest were woods and cliffs—seemed all of one piece, despite its disparate parts.

In back, the chapel led into the grounds. Several arches curled over the path out to the soccer field—this was part of some previous owner's dream, an ancient bit of wall and arch brought over from Europe at a time when overly moneyed men did such things.

To the west of all this were the dull brick buildings that included the middle school classrooms, the science lab, the language lab, and the art studio that had only just been added within the past two years. Beyond these, nearly a quarter mile across the track and bleachers, was the Field House, where the swimming pool and basketball court were housed, and which doubled as a theater when the students from Harrow and the neighboring St. Catherine's School for Girls did their once-a-year play.

To the east, what had once been a caretaker's cottage had sprouted and grown into the Trenches, which was simply another way of saying the dormitories for upper school boys. Another more brickish building stood just behind it, called Heights, which held the rest of the boys that attended Harrow.

A total of 150 students attended Harrow in any given year, for it was small and exclusive and intended to remain that way as far as the headmaster was concerned; few classrooms held more than ten or twelve students at a time; it was one of the draws for parents who wanted their boys to get a real education. It was old-fashioned, another draw: Latin was a requirement for graduation, as was Theology and a brief course in Greek. Being an all-boys school, it harkened back for many to a simpler time, and had such a British air about it that Mr. Duvall, the Latin teacher, had begun to speak in cadences not unlike a member of the House of Lords.

It was the reason that Harrow could charge such an outrageous rate for tuition and board. No student, it was presumed, left the narrow halls of the Great House, as the main house was called, without having received a first-class education, a sense of purpose, and a highly developed moral code based on honor and hard work.

At least, this was what the brochure put forth.

This was the goal of Harrow, and had been since the school began its existence.

It was the reason Jim's father had gone there, and why his brother had, also.

And now that they were dead, it was up to him.

The saying above The Great Door of the school (everything in Harrow seemed to be called The Great Something) was simple: *Journey with Us into Enlightenment, and Wait for What Will Come*.

The beginning of James Cambell Hook's journey to enlightenment occurred one autumn day, in the unlikeliest of places.

6

Of course the school had a history, as everything does. Before it was a school, it was someone's house, it's supposed; and before that owner, another, and before him, even another.

It was said in Watch Point that the man who built the original house may in fact have done something terrible, once upon a time. There was even a man who lived in Watch Point—a very old, nearly feeble man, whose weight had dropped rapidly over the past year, whose eyesight was no longer able to distinguish beyond form and shadow, and whose time was, perhaps, at hand—and he had just remarked to his nurse the summer previous that, "Crowley used to tell me it was the most awful place."

His nurse, a young woman of twenty-three, glanced up from her chair. "Mr. Palliser?"

"He used to tell me that it wouldn't rest. He used to tell me that seven were too many," the man said, and then he leaned forward to whisper something in the young woman's ear.

Later, when the breath had left the old man, the young woman was not sure that his last words should bear repeating.

But of course, for Jim Hook, then a boy of fifteen, all of this went unnoticed.

He was, after all, in love, only he was the last to know.

Sometimes, life is all about the wrong place at the wrong time.

Chapter Four
The Night Before

1

Jim held her, leaning back in the crunchy pile of fallen leaves. The leaves sighed under their combined weight, and he felt leaf stickers in his side and maybe a rock or two somewhere in there—but he didn't mind.

It was a crispy night, crackling and sputtering like a live wire laid out on the sleepiest town in the world. A heavy dampness hung in the air like rain was about to come down, and it was October and he could practically taste life in the back of his throat, delicious life, like he hadn't tasted in months, perhaps even years.

And it was because of this girl, this Lark Trot-

Douglas Clegg

ter, this Junior at St. Catherine's, with her warm arms and cool glances and bursting laughs.

There was a marshy smell to the air—but it wasn't unpleasant, it was the Hudson River, just beyond the next rise; he could see the lights on the other side of it, and he wondered if the world on that side felt as good as he did on this side right now.

Right now.

With his girl there, with the world seeming to be full of nothing but possibilities, with the night so . . . *prosperous*. That was the only word that came to his mind. It was a night of wealth for him—not cheap money, but the wealth of feeling like a kid his age with a pretty girl in his arms and no worries beyond the moment.

Lark Trotter. His girl.

She felt like warmth personified, her breath was heat, her eyes were fire, her smile—well, his sense of metaphor ended when he saw spit fly from her lips as she laughed. Lark Trotter. Even her name got him smiling. *Even her name*, he thought. *Everything about her*.

"Jim!" she shouted, laughing. Lark had an adorable laugh, even with the spit; what was so funny? Did it matter? She was there, with him. That's all that mattered.

"Lark!" he laughed back, and kissed her ear and then her hair and then his lips met hers in their twenty-fifth official kiss (yes, he was counting). He felt the stickers poking through his sweater, smelled the stinky wet leaf mold all around them.

She pulled back, and sat up.

The misty blue night had descended, and with it a gentle chill. They'd spent the evening at the movies, then what they had both quickly termed the Great Pup Caper, then had gone to the all-night coffee shop at Frigg and Burnside, and if it was after midnight, he didn't care, she didn't care, it was fun just hanging out with each other.

She straightened her sweater and looked down at him. She was pretty to him even though she wasn't in the cheerleader mold that the other boys tended to fall all over—she looked smart and kind, and perhaps even devious in a good way, that charmed him completely. Her eyes were cinnamon coffee. Her breath was minty fresh, which he had joked about with her on their first kiss, and she had replied, "Better than that sour milk of your breath," and he immediately had wanted to run off to brush his teeth because he'd felt so bad, but she had just laughed and told him not to worry because she had some spearmint gum for him.

He had known then that she actually liked him.

He was still surprised that she liked him at all, but it felt right.

"It's getting late. I need to get back some-

51

time before dawn." She yawned and shivered slightly. Her face was half in shadow and half beneath the streetlamp, which seemed to pour its shine across her features.

He liked just looking at her. He liked the way he felt when he looked at her, when she was smiling. When she seemed to keep some secret from him. "It must be nearly one. Too late to stay out. If my R.A. discovers this, I'm gonna be in trouble for the next six weeks. Alice Garver lost weekends last year because she got caught. She had to spend the whole time at Mrs. Farrell's house, and I can tell you, that in itself would be worth committing suicide over."

"Just another minute. Or ten," he said.

He crossed his arms behind his head and gazed up at her. Man, she was cute. Lark Trotter. The strangest name—it conjured up images of someone taking a small bird out for a run. But on her, the name was perfect, it sounded like . . . like . . . music, he thought.

And she was sweet—kind, generous, helpful. Could he think enough good about her? Half the reason they were out so late was because of that damn dog.

The Great Pup Caper, to be precise.

2

Someone had nearly run down a yellow Labrador retriever puppy at the corner of Jackson and Rhone, and Lark immediately called the local vet, and wouldn't even leave the animal hospital until she was sure the dog was well cared for.

The puppy was stunned, although only its front left paw seemed to actually have any damage. The animal was squealing and bleeding, and Lark had tugged off the wool scarf that hung around her neck and swathed the damaged paw up in it. She even hated parting with the puppy when the vet's assistant took it into one of the operating rooms.

Jim had been with her the whole time—and even if it was annoying to have spent three hours of their Sunday together sitting in a vet's waiting room hanging in there for the prognosis of a little ball of yellow fur that hadn't even seemed particularly grateful, it made him like her all the more.

Then, they'd both lost track of time, and had wandered the streets of Watch Point, knowing they were breaking curfew, but not caring, not worrying, not noticing anything but how much fun it was to be together.

3

Lark was smart, too, and she could even be cruel sometimes when she wanted to be—it was what he liked about her. She never let him off the hook. He could imagine her younger, telling the kids on a playground that what they were doing was bad. He could imagine her giving that look to him, the look that meant he was being "such a boy."

She didn't like being taken for granted. She was completely cool.

Dark hair, sparkling eyes, and all the good stuff girls had going for them—all of it was right there in Lark, Lark, Lark, and it was just great to hang with her, let alone make out.

"Jenny would laugh at me right now, you know."

"No she wouldn't."

"Yes she would. I'm a junior, you're a sophomore," Lark said in a mock-imperious voice. "You can't imagine how wrong that is. The boy is meant to be older."

"That's so . . . so . . ."

"1953," Lark finished it for him.

"Yeah!"

"The year my mother was born." Lark leaned back on one elbow. "She went to St. Cat's, too. She met Dad here when she was seventeen."

"Ah," Jim quieted. He closed his eyes for a moment and thought of what it would be like to feel Lark's body against his without the barrier of clothes. He was nearly embarrassed that he was thinking of her breasts so much; he saw her as more innocent than those lustful thoughts, but she'd given him more than a clue while they'd been making out that the relationship could go further at some point soon.

He wanted her body. All right, he could admit it to himself. He liked her, and lusted after her. He lusted after a lot of girls—he had since he was eleven and had begun to feel stirrings beyond the mental kind. There were plenty of girls at St. Cat's and Valley Catholic School and The Hope School who were hot and cute and fun, and fueled brief fantasies, but Lark was all of it. It was all there at once. He wasn't going to mention this to her, and he felt too awkward to be aggressive. It was enough just to have the movie in his brain. He imagined them both naked, and his hands on her breasts, and their lips together.

Then, he opened his eyes to watch her again. She was everything: pure and sexual and sweet and dark and smart and inviting and . . . what else? He couldn't think of all the things she was. He was falling fast. He wanted her badly; but he was too awkward to go beyond a sweet kiss. He didn't think nice boys or nice girls did much beyond that anyway, although half the boys at school talked as if everyone did all the time and in every which way.

Lark was different. And fun. And wild. And sweet. She even had her down side, and that got to him all the more. She could be moody. She got pissed off sometimes over things that seemed inconsequential to him. Once, she was angry for an entire day because he had forgotten to call her when he'd said he would. He still didn't understand it, but he knew that she was worth apologizing to if he had an inkling that he might've screwed up somehow.

And now—here. With him. "A great day," he sighed, not realizing he was expressing it aloud.

"I'll bet you never had a bad day in your life," she said.

"What?" he chuckled.

"You just seem happy."

"No, I'm dark and mysterious," he asserted, lowering his voice; his laugh gave him away.

"You don't have a dark side," she insisted. "You're sunny and confident."

"My dark side is . . . is . . ." he thought a second. "My dark side has got to be that I don't have a dark side."

"That's what I thought," she sighed. "I think we need to develop some sorrow and pain in you."

"Ah," he said, trying not to let his tone change. He didn't want her to see any other side to him than the fun-loving one, the kind that girls wanted to see in boys.

"I have a deep dark secret," she volunteered.

"And that is?"

She held her breath a moment and then burst out laughing. "I suck at math."

"Well," he said, "that's mine too. And I suck at Latin. Although my pig latin is ite-quay errific-tay."

"You are such a geek, Jim. Why am I dating

a guy who actually will say words in pig latin?" She slapped him playfully on the shoulder. "Look at the river," she said, leaning forward. "It's best here in fall. I hate the winters and springs, but the falls here are worth it."

"Fall. Fell. Fallen," he whispered.

"Jim?"

"Just how I'm feeling right now."

"Oh you."

"Oh me oh my."

"Stop mocking me, James," she said. She picked a couple of crumbling leaves up and tossed them on his face.

He spat out leaf bits. "What is it about all this?"

"Huh?"

"Being here. Out so late we can see all the lights across the Hudson. They're like diamonds or something. And coffee in my blood. And we rescued a puppy. And the moon. God, look at that moon! And . . . with you. Knowing I have to get back to Harrow. Knowing you have to get back to St. Cat's. Wouldn't it be great if we could go to our own place?"

"Yeah, in about a decade. Please."

"I meant it in a nice way."

"I know," she said. "I meant it in a nice way, too. I dated a boy once who wouldn't have meant it in a nice way."

"Yeah, well, I'm not Charlie Cornwall."

57

"I'm not saying you are. Do you see him much?" she asked.

The question irked him. "Sometimes. In phys ed. He's not a bad guy."

"Boys love boys like that. It's girls who have to watch out."

"Let's not talk about him, okay?" Jim said testily.

"Okay. I didn't mean to bring him up. I'm just glad I don't have to run into him anymore."

"No, you don't. I'm here."

"I know," she said, sounding embarrassed. "I just wish you'd kick him in the balls sometime."

"Ha," Jim said.

"I should never date you boys at Harrow."

"Come here, you," he said.

"No, you."

He sat up and leaned into her, kissing her gently. Then it began to rain, and they had to leap up and run through the downpour. Something within him told him that he didn't want this moment to end.

4

Watch Point was a town of a few thousand residents, most of them scattered around the gently sloping hills, its streets running in rivulets between village homes that were severe, austere, and nearly like peasant cottages from some medieval hour; others, more modern, just around the periphery of town, were built by summer people who rarely visited once Labor Day had passed.

The character of Watch Point had not changed in nearly a century—it was the same sleepy little hamlet it had always been, far enough off the beaten track from the more popular towns of the Hudson Valley, and what wasn't hamlet was woods, and rising from among the thickest of the woods, the School, as it was known to the locals.

Some townies called it "that damn preppie hotel."

In the rain, Watch Point seemed like a runny watercolor of a place, with mismatched shops and brackish storefronts with antique crap and the fire department with its stable and the old barn behind the glass factory—and Jim ran with his arm around Lark until they'd reached the train station down on Corday Street, by the KrumCo parking lot.

Brief memories of their first few dates in town were always there for him, and passing the firehouse, he remembered his first kiss with Lark back in April, and how sex flashed in his mind briefly, and then turned to a kind of warmth as their lips unlocked, and then turned to nervousness when he knew he wanted to kiss her again; the railroad tracks were their first long walk together, holding hands; and one Sunday Lark had come up to visit and they'd

59

actually gone to church at Grace, the Episcopal Church over at Lantern Square; in the rain, the memories bled together.

They stood beneath the eaves of the depot, waiting for the one A.M. train—the last that would take her back to Cold Spring and St. Catherine's School for Girls ("School for Wayward Girls," he would tease her sometimes); she leaned against his shoulder, shivering, which only made him hug her a little tighter to try to warm her; and he thought, as they waited, that something was so sweet about rushing to not get caught, about waiting for trains, about staying warm together.

Then he remembered his exam.

The following day. Third period.

Western Civ.

"You'll do fine," Lark said, before grasping his hand for a last quick squeeze before boarding the train.

"I hope so."

"Aw, Jimmy, it's not like you haven't been studying since the beginning of term for this," she said, and then she was on the train. "Now get back to the Trenches before you get reamed by Harkness. Don't forget about the puppy. We need to make sure we find its home. I'll pay the vet bill."

"No, I will," he insisted.

"No, I will," she ignored his words. "My mother cries when a rat gets killed in a trap.

She'll shell out the money and probably end up with her third dog through this. Don't worry. Just make sure you check on the pup this week, and we'll figure it out from there."

"Yeah," he nodded, and then she was on the train before he could get a last kiss in.

He waved goodbye and laughed at himself for worrying about a midterm, even though the course was Western Civ and he didn't understand the Crusades at all, and he really hadn't been doing enough studying in that one subject since the beginning of the term.

He knew he was screwed.

Chapter Five
Lark, on the Train

Lark Trotter settled into her seat on the train and glanced out into the darkness.

She practically tore her heavy wool sweater off and dumped it near her feet; she slipped out of her shoes, wiggling her toes, which were cold and wet from rain. It felt good to stretch out a bit. If she could have, she would have just stretched out and probably fallen asleep right on the train and missed her stop and ended up in Manhattan.

She was that exhausted. All she could think about was her eight o'clock class, and the fact that she hadn't read all of the assignment for French, even though she figured she could fake it if it were absolutely necessary. And getting by the House Mother and the Resident Adviser back at St. Cat's—that would be a near impossibility, but if she got Beth Mobley to just open her window a little so she could crawl in and then sneak back down to her room, she might just get away with it. The various thoughts spun around in her head, conjuring images of doom, tests, and sleep.

Don't conk out. Not yet. You can put in at least a half hour once you're back looking over the textbook. Then you can sleep for—what—four and a half hours?

Yikes.

I should've had some tea, damn it. Maybe Jenny has some coffee. I could just pull an all-nighter, what the heck.

Someone had left a folded-up *New York Times* in the seatback pouch. She drew it out and flipped through it, hoping the crossword puzzle would be intact, but someone had sadistically taken a pen to it. It was a half hour back to St. Catherine's, and she was trying to figure out just how she was going to bribe her roommate, Marti, to not get her in trouble with Mrs. Starnes, when she noticed the man.

He wore a fairly unfashionable gray hat, and a rain slicker.

He sat directly across from her. He kept leaning forward and staring at her.

She didn't look at him directly, but instead caught a glimpse of him from the corner of her eye. At first she ignored his strange attention, but within a few minutes, she grew tired of the slight annoyance.

Finally, Lark turned to the stranger, figuring a good glare would let him know how rude he was to ogle her, but the seat was empty.

Chapter Six
The Headmaster, at Home

1

Her fingers reaching for him; violently, she tossed her head back as she sat down against his hips; the lights flashed on and off and he saw her breasts. . . .

Jay Trimalchio, just shy of forty-six but feeling all of eighteen from a very erotic dream, thought he heard someone call his name. He roiled like a storm cloud in some kind of flashing blue light—in his dream—with a woman as beautiful and endless as the sea, her hair wild like a horse's mane, her breasts as large and round as honeydews but soft as sponges, and her hips riding his at a reckless gallop. He bucked against her; she felt moist as the sea on a summer day, surrounding all of him; and her legs were all over him, all around his back, and she was nothing but legs and breasts, and her hair swept down his face—

But someone called his name again.

He yawned himself out of the dream slowly, still feeling the magic fingers of the imaginary woman with the silken hair that grazed his chest—at two in the morning no less, as he noticed the green glow of the digital alarm clock by his bedside—to see what seemed to be a fire outside the window of his town house that overlooked the Big Clock of Watch Point.

He was, of course, alone, in his bunched-up boxers, and the thought of a fire made his throat go dry.

No one had called his name, leastwise not the person that immediately came to mind when he tried to remember the voice.

Jacky, that wiseass. His voice full of spit and vinegar, and some scheme to break into the dining hall, way back when, back in the days when Trimalchio broke into things and got in trouble for it.

Fire. He practically heard someone say the word.

Fire.

Trimalchio's heart raced, and he sat up in bed, only to find that there was no fire at all—it was merely an optical illusion of the flashing yellow of the streetlight against the window of the building directly across from his, and his overactive imagination. He glanced around the shadowy room, and then out into the night. Rain droplets remained on his window; the yellow light still wavering.

Well, you're awake now. . . . He rolled more than rose from his rumpled bed, and wobbled on unsteady feet to the stairs—made less steady by a couple of pints down at the Coach & Four—to make his way to the kitchen, scratching his butt with each step down.

Flicked the light up. It came on brilliant, strong, and brought with it a powerful headache.

In the kitchen, he opened the fridge, thinking some of the leftover Kung Pao chicken might just hit the spot. After devouring a bit of this, he went to take a leak, and that's when he found the dead mouse floating in the toilet.

2

It was a bit sad.

Jay had known that the mouse lived somewhere in his house. He had even put out breadcrumbs and cheese for it, but for some suicidal reason, the mouse had chosen that evening to end it all by drowning in the scummy bowl. *To flush or not to flush? Christ, I can't pee on it. Not while it's floating there. Looking pathetic. Poor mouse.*

After scooping the waterlogged mouse up and tossing it in the plastic trash bag by the door, and then finally taking his longed-for leak, Trimalchio went to his desk at the front window and switched on his computer. His mug of the previous morning's coffee—some of it still curdled within—sat beside the ashtray filled with the gray remains of his pipe. He reached for the pouch of chocolate tobacco, unrolled it; then took a bit out and stuffed it down into his pipe. Lighting it, he pressed it between his lips and closed his eyes for a moment. At least something was good. At least he had his pipe.

After all, he wasn't going to be getting any sleep.

The night was shot.

He tended toward sound sleep if he dropped off before eleven, but had found over the years that if he stayed awake much after midnight, he would be up most of the night.

Headmasters rarely did well on a few hours' sleep a night. But sometimes, he just had to face a cold Monday morning without his usual eight hours. He booted up his computer, played a game of hearts and three of solitaire, and then decided to go online and see if there was any good porn to be had.

It wasn't an obsession. But since Daisy (yes, Daisy, as insane as it had seemed to date a woman named Daisy at all) had taken off—no, she had leaped from him like he was a car about to crash—two years earlier, he had found that he didn't want to get involved in the flesh again. At least not for a while. But the occasional fantasy via modem was not a bad way to pass the hours of loneliness.

He tried some of his favorite sites, but watching other men fondle women, all of them strangers to him, was beginning to seem silly. *You're not eighteen. You're too old for this kind of game. Good Christ, Jay. You've confiscated this kind of stuff from the students at school. It's like you're back in Harrow as a kid rather than running the place. Get on with your pathetic existence.*

He clicked his mouse over to check his email.

His sister had written from Boston, but with no news to speak of other than some bitterness over the whole inheritance issue, which pissed him off to the point that he had to delete the note in midsentence rather than read the whole thing; and his old friend Tom had dropped him a joke from his law practice email address; and then there was some spam about "Great Opportunities in Home Business," and "Sexy Girls Go All Night Long," which he promptly deleted, unread. Then, an email with his own return address, with the subject: TRIMALCHIO I'M BACK.

Confused, assuming this was some kind of spam, he opened the note.

For a second, his screen went black, and then came up again.

The letter read:

Sport,

After twenty years, you haven't changed.

Neither have I.

Yes, it's me, you knew I'd come back again to check up on you. That's why you've remained behind, isn't it? Never sure just when I'd be making my reappearance, but you knew somehow I would. Didn't you? And you'll never guess exactly what brought me back, but it won't matter.

What matters is, I want to see you again. Yes, even after it all, I want to see you where you know you'll find me. Where you've always been able to find me, if only you would open the door and step inside.

The crazy part about this, Sport, is that you really want to see me, too, don't you? You've always wanted to, only you can't face it. Well, face it, Sport, we're like glue, and you've never really gone that far from me, have you? I've always been here, waiting.

See you soon.

All my best,
The Jackal

72

3

Trimalchio went over to the small bar near his TV set and poured some Johnny Walker Red into a glass, went to the freezer to add some ice cubes, and took his drink back to the computer.

He sat down, puffed some more on his pipe, tried to imagine what it all meant, and drank more than a sip from the glass. The whiskey was warm and smooth. He glanced out the window, at his Ford Explorer, and the flashing yellow streetlight down the block; at the wavering silence of the street.

Then he looked back at the computer screen.

He read the email a few times, trying to figure out who could play this kind of trick—or who *would* play it—when he realized that the original email address was not his personal one, but was sent by his work email. It would have to be a student playing a prank.

Probably from the library computers, or from one of their own laptops.

That was it.

Some student had hacked his way into a teacher's email address and was using it.

Trimalchio resolved to get to the bottom of it the following day.

But still, something within the note had touched him, and it took all of his strength not to remember that night, many years before, when he had watched his best friend die right before his eyes.

Chapter Seven
In the Trenches

1

At Harrow, the Trenches had once been the groundskeeper's cottage, and still bore the original caretaker's name: *Oliver Palliser*, carved into the white stone at its entrance.

Hardly a cottage, it was three times as big as the first house Jim had lived in; it housed thirty-five students on four different floors, in small, Spartan rooms, two beds apiece, one sink, one mirror (often cracked), one closet, and one slim window. The housemaster was Mr. Crowe, first floor middle—an extended apartment that even had its own can. Crowe was the most irresponsible housemaster of them all—when he wasn't off with his fiancée in some motel along the roadside, he was sacked out by ten o'clock at night with a combination of martinis and Sominex, so the Trenches and its orderliness, or lack thereof, was pretty much up to the resident advisers.

Lights Out started at ten and went till eleven, but it was ignored whenever exams were in the air; and as long as no one raised a ruckus, the various housemasters and the two house mothers who lived on campus let a lot go on if no one got into trouble.

But still, it was 2 A.M.

This might mean twenty demerits, which might mean running around the track twenty times and clearing the rocks and pebbles from the soccer field and having mandatory detention on Saturday and Sunday mornings and no weekend pass until Christmas.

It could be that bad.

2

Jim was one of six students in the basement dorms.

The first floor held the two resident advisers' rooms—they were seniors named Harkness and Beeker, although the boys in the Trenches called them Hardass and Bleeder; in addition, four juniors shared rooms on the main floor.

Then, the second and third stories held the

broom closet rooms for the remaining twenty-two students. The floors were creaky, the only entrances were on the main floor, and it was hard to get through the doors or windows without making enough noise to alert Hardass and Bleeder.

Jim looked at the window into the bathroom, but the last time he'd snuck back in that way, he'd ended up surprising Clifton, who was on the can, and who cried out just as Jim had slipped down on the tile floor, narrowly escaping a concussion.

This time, it was either the front door or the back door.

Hardass lived near the front; Bleeder near the back. Hardass's light was out; Bleeder's still burned.

Jim walked around the house and peered into Bleeder's open window. The blinds were only partially shut, torn and ragged near the bottom, and he got a glimpse of Bleeder.

Bleeder was gawky and buck-toothed, but he stank of money and this naturally helped him find some acceptance among the more opportunistic boys. He was not the smartest of seniors, nor was he popular in the least, but he had the most extensive collection of porn in the entire school, and there he was, lifting up a picture of an orgy—some tangle of flesh that Jim could not quite make out—and reaching into his underwear with his free hand. Jim turned away from the window, trying to not to picture the rest of this scenario.

All right, he thought. *Getting past Bleeder's room will be simple*.

It was anything but simple, because as soon as Jim turned the knob on the back door, and had pulled it wide enough to slip in, he saw Hardass in his big white nightshirt and checkered boxers coming out of the bathroom, flicking lights up as he went. Hardass, chubby and freckled and eternally scowling because he was having trouble getting through his last year at the 'Row, glanced down the narrow hall at the open door.

Jim froze in the doorway.

Hardass lumbered toward him, the floorboards groaning, and Jim nearly wanted to laugh because Hardass had bunny slippers on his feet, but Hardass's scowl grew into a full-fledged pissed-offedness. "What the hell are you doing, Hook?" His voice like curdled milk in the throat of a newborn calf.

Jim caught his breath for a second. *Think. Think.* It wouldn't be enough to just be wandering on campus. Curfew was at ten, sometimes it could be stretched to eleven, but after one A.M. it was damn suspect.

"I needed to take a leak," Jim volunteered. "You were in the bathroom. So I just went out and, you know . . ."

"Oh, hell yeah," Hardass said. "And what's

78

wrong with the one in your quarters?"

"Meloni was in it."

"Like I believe you. There's second and third floor, too. Three urinals on second. What, was everyone taking a crap at the precise moment your bladder was exploding? A little bird told me you were off with some Cat-House girl to-night. Maybe you were out with her and maybe you're just sneaking in."

"I guess you'll believe what you want to be-lieve."

"Two demerits, Hook. Toilet duty for two weeks or Senior slave for one month. Your choice."

Jim shook his head. At Harrow, you accepted the small punishments; he had seen one boy go against the system, and that kid had ended up getting booted. This wasn't an option for Jim. "I guess toilets are it."

"Good. I want them sparkling. Use your toothbrush if you have to," Hardass said, and then grinned. He looked like a jack-o'-lantern.

I'll use your *toothbrush to get the toilets shiny*, Jim wanted to say, but was content to think it, and instead nodded to Hardass, and told him that of course he was right and it wouldn't hap-pen again.

"It's not good to lie," Hardass added, like a kick in the butt. "Lying fucks you over. I bet that brother of yours never lied."

79

Douglas Clegg

3

Jim entered his room like a prisoner heading for death row. The week had already begun in the shitter and was moving swiftly toward the sewer, and it was only just the dark side of Monday morning.

Jim glanced at Mojo Meloni, hunched over his laptop on his bed, books and papers spread around.

Mojo was a train wreck of a preppie—his khakis were nearly threadbare because he only ever wore one pair over and over again. His Izod shirts, passed down from his father's golfing days, were two sizes too big for him. Like Jim, he was on scholarship, but was naturally book-smart and wise in the ways of handling Harrow in a manner that Jim knew he himself would never be. "Glad you're up. Mojo, you got notes from Civ?"

"Hell no. Kelleher spouts stupid crap. I use this," Mojo said, tapping away at his laptop's keyboard. The laptop was an overnight check-out from the library, one of twenty that could be reserved by students.

Mojo always kept the laptop checked out over the return date, knowing that the librarian wouldn't fine him because she believed his family was poverty-stricken, when in fact Mojo's dad probably could've paid for tuition and board, only—in Mojo's words—"My dad knows how to work the system. You gotta know how to work the system, Jimmy Jammy, you gotta work that mother."

His hair was wild all over his scalp, a nest of viperous blond straw. Thin headphones thrust beside his ears with the tinny sound of Garbage playing. "If it weren't for AOL, I'd be up the friggin' creek. I found seven sources for the Crusades."

"Print it out for me?"

"Printer crapped out. You want, I can bookmark it."

"Okay. It help much?"

Mojo let out a fierce guffaw that was half sneeze and half laugh. "Let me put it this way: I knew squat about the Byzantines and the whole damn Saladin business. And then I logged on and started a Yahoo search and pretty soon, voila. But man, it's nearly 2 A.M. You are screwed. How'd you get past the guards?"

"Bleeder was wanking and Hardass got me. I got crapper duty for a while."

"Hardass sucks." Mojo nodded. "He had that kid from third, you know, the one with the corkscrew nose, he had him practically licking out the toilet. It was majorly disgusting. Undignified. Christ. All this money they all spend to go to boot camp." Then he put his headphones back on and continued tip-tapping on the keys.

Jim sat down on his bed and told himself he was going to just close his eyes for a second.

And he did. He sat back against his two pillows, closed his eyes, and tried to imagine the Crusades, but nothing came to him. He thought of a sword, and then a cross and crescent, and then the sack of Jerusalem. But no images came.

Instead, he thought of Lark and the way she had kissed him, and he imagined himself drawing her sweater over her head, and pretty soon, something within himself told him to open his eyes or he was going to flunk the Western Civ midterm; but then, there was Lark saying, "Oh, Jim, you don't need to study. You're so smart. You're my smart, wonderful studly boyfriend," and then she wasn't Lark at all but some tarted-up vixen in thigh-high boots and laced red bodice, and her hair had gone completely honey-blond, and pretty soon it went from being a dream to a wet dream. But somewhere in the depths of the dream, he was in the old house in Bronxville, and he was looking up at the attic door. Someone was knocking on the other side of the door.

Someone was scraping at it.

It was as if a wild animal had gotten trapped in the attic.

Scratching at the door.

The scratches increased in frequency.

Coming through.

He was a boy of eleven again. It was the night his brother and father had died, and he stood before the attic door, and something terrible was about to break out from behind it.

The next thing he knew, Mojo was shaking him awake, his eyes stung, his tongue felt like parchment, his breath stank, his brain hurt from the hint of sunlight that came through the window, and he was hoping that this new moment was the dream.

"Hey bud," Mojo said. "You got a class in twenty minutes. I think you might want to shower, fart-face."

Fifteen was an age of tyrants and victims, the hormonally challenged and the hormonally advanced.

Somewhere, in between it all, Jim found himself in a hellish situation. It didn't help that his ties seemed to have disappeared in the night, that his shirt, starched as of Saturday, was lying, wrinkled, on the closet floor, and that something that looked dangerously like dog crap was on the heel of his shoes.

But they were omens for him, in some strange way.

Omens of the worst day to come.

Chapter Eight
The Day Begins

1

Some losers routinely got up at 5 A.M. to jog three miles around town and then shower at the field house to get to their desks and delve into their work so that they'd be fresh and brilliant for the young minds as they poured into the classrooms, but Gert McTeague was having none of it.

She always got up just ten minutes before she was due in the headmaster's office—at eight A.M.—and sometimes she managed to shower and do her hair in that short period of time, sometimes she didn't, but if anyone complained, she would deck them with a glare that was famous at Harrow Academy, and had been since she'd worked under Old Man Chambers back in the 1960s, her first years at the school as Upper School Secretary.

Gert sometimes stank of nightsweat and whatever garlic-laden meat she'd been mixing with her beer, but what she lacked in hygiene she made up for in warmth—at least, according to her—and when she arrived at the Main Office at eight that morning, she was surprised to see that Trimalchio had not beat her to it. She unlocked the office door and switched on the lights.

But something was not quite right.

Sure, everything was in place, she'd later tell her friend Sally, who worked in the supply storeroom; sure, the front area looked as neat as it had the day before; the switchboard, old-fashioned dinosaur that it was, hadn't been gummed up with chewing gum, as the class of '76 had done one spring day; and nothing seemed to be missing from her desk.

But something was off.

Finally, she noticed what it was: Someone had taken all the plaques and framed photographs off the wall and had switched their positions. The picture of the school was where the photo of the headmaster should have been; the photo of Old Man Chambers was now in the place where the original sketch of Harrow Academy had been.

"It wasn't anything worth losing sanity over," she told Sally on her third cigarette break of the morning, "but why would any of these kids take the time to do something as ridiculous as that? Ridiculous."

"Because they're like that," Sally said, sucking back on a menthol stick. "They're all a bunch of sociopaths, you ask me."

2

In the boiler room, the janitor, a man of fifty-seven named Seth Oaks, who had nearly been fired seven years running, looked at what was painted on the wall near the furnace. He was thinking of reporting it, but was sure that he'd just get threatened again, merely because he sometimes drank too much on the job—as if it were anyone's business.

The words were, even to his mind, *obscene*, and he worked half the morning scrubbing them away so that no one would ever see them.

3

Joey Cippola was always the first kid in first period Latin III, and when he got into class that morning, he recognized the words written on the blackboard. At first, he thought it was going to be the lesson, but as he translated the words as best he could, it bothered him more than he thought something so simple-minded ever could.

The words translated to:

BE HE ALIVE OR BE HE DEAD.

4

Mr. Potts and Mrs. Custer were rumored to be having an affair, although no one could have ever matched a more unlikely pair.

There was a certain ratlike quality to both of them, and in some ways they looked as if they'd come from the same gene pool—they were on the short side, and Mr. Potts was a bit hunched over, paunchy, while Mrs. Custer was broad-shouldered, straight-backed, and husky but not soft. Yet it was their eyes, their round brown eyes, and the slightly pugged noses they both possessed; and perhaps something in the way Custer walked that shared the same rhythm with Potts's wobbling march. Although they had first names—William and Adele—they called each other Potts and Custer and would not even allow contemporaries to call them by anything else.

And yes, the rumors were true.

They had been sharing quarters in town for nearly twenty years, while maintaining separate residences because there was a clause in the teachers' contracts about romantic relationships between staff members.

Mischief

Potts was the head of the Computer Department and the Math Club, and Custer ran the language lab and taught first-year French. There was something so alike about these two, it seemed criminal that they should wake up in the mornings in each other's beefy arms, and somewhat perverted that they should spend two decades hiding a secret that was obvious to even the youngest of the boys.

After their morning pollutions, as Custer called the ritual of the bath, the toilet, and the morning razor, Potts would sneak out the back door of Custer's little ground-floor apartment, and quickly grab a *Morning Post* from the newsstand that Mitch Liu ran on the other side of the fire station across the street. Potts kept the pretense up even for the townies of Watch Point, and Custer would wait a decent ten minutes, and then open her front door and walk up three steps to the street level, all fresh and squeezed into a conservative smock of a suit, her briefcase by her side. She'd wave to Potts, who, across the street, would nod back to her, and then call to her and ask if she cared for coffee; she routinely said no.

It was every day, this performance they had for the uninterested townspeople; and then she would walk up the street, climbing the drive to the school; Potts would arrive several minutes later. Should they pass in the hall, one would pretend the other did not exist.

This particular morning, they rose and separated as usual, and when Custer, her hair pulled back in a French twist, stepped into the room designated as the language lab, with its tape players and headphones, and rows of tapes, records, CDs, and videos stored on shelves along the wall, she hadn't expected to find a boy hanging by a noose from the large beam that ran the length of the room.

5

Custer swallowed hard, a million thoughts going through her head; taking the boy down was not one of them. Neither was calling out for help. Instead, she knew what she must do.

She stepped back out of the language lab, and closed the door, then locked it. She glanced up and down the hall. It was still morning-empty.

The students had not yet begun wandering in slowly from the field or dining hall. She walked down the corridor, trying not to picture what she had just seen—

His eyes, bulging—

Tongue, hanging out—

His face, completely blue—

And now, in her memory, was he trying to say something? Were his lips moving? But it was just in her mind. That's all. It didn't happen. He was just hanging there.

6

When she found Potts, already hunched over his gigantic computer monitor and keyboard, tap-tapping away at some program he claimed to be creating that would change the software industry forever, the first thing out of her mouth was, "Potts, I think I'm out of luck."

Potts managed to calm her, managed to coax the keys to the language lab from her, and wobbled down the corridor ahead of her, muttering to himself. She'd catch up with him every few feet and mutter something about "boy" and "strangled" and "noose" and "dangling," but Potts was unclear as to just what she meant. They passed Angstrom, nervously bounding down to his own office as if a bomb were about to explode, and when Potts set the key into the lock, Custer grabbed his hand.

"It's terrible," she muttered. "Just gawdawful." Tears began squeezing from the edges of her eyelids, and her hands were shaking just like when she'd gone too many days without coffee.

Potts opened the door, and looked around the room. "Custer? You imagining things?" He chortled a bit too much, which annoyed her when he did it, and she knew that he wouldn't remind her that she may have had a few too many martinis the previous night and not enough food.

Douglas Clegg

Custer, unable to look in the room again, a room which did not hold a boy hanging from a rope, began shivering.

Because the face of the boy had become clearer in her mind.

She had known him.

Chapter Nine
The Baddest of Days

1

It started after gym class, the Baddest of Days, in the locker room, where all bad things in high school tend to originate.

The shower steam had not yet faded, and the morning light filtered through the high translucent windows like something that the chaplain called "a Jesus moment." The quality of light, within the mist, was quite beautiful and golden, and gave a sepia tint to the half-naked boys running, slipping, pacing in what one of the teachers called "the smelliest locker room this side of the dump." The smells were socks and jocks and Nikes and New Balance shoes that burst with teenaged boy foot stink like flowers in some horrifying springtime; and someone hadn't flushed the toilet in stall number three in days because Skipper Fleet had sworn it was the biggest dump he had ever seen in his life and was sure the janitor had done it; and between the steam and the stink and the shouts, it was a hassle and a half to get showered, changed, dried, and ready for third period, and at least one of the seventh graders was complaining about how he was going to catch pneumonia if he didn't get his hair dry. That Warner kid, who was really weird, had his towel all the way up to his armpits; and everybody and his brother were cracking jokes about it.

The noise was wicked loud, the shouts and calls, and then there was Bilge, whose real name was Billy G. Shea, who refused to take his gym clothes off to shower, whining that he was at Harrow for education and to prepare for college, not to get naked in front of a bunch of jocks; so Bilge and Coach Wright were shouting at each other from the glassed-in office; and Shrike Boucher tormented the seventh graders who had just begun the process of showering off from a muddy morning out on the soccer field.

Shrike had his jockstrap over his head, and began rat-tailing the first seventh grader who came running out of the shower. "It's a ritual, worms, your first year of showers, you need a little butt-kicking!"

2

Jim Hook was just spinning the combination on his lock, wondering why he hadn't prepared for the midterm, and mentally kicking himself for spending half the weekend with Lark. He almost blamed her and then he blamed himself and then he blamed that damn puppy that they had to rescue, but the truth hit him square in the face.

It didn't matter what he had done on the weekend. He still would not have been ready for the midterm, because he had barely stayed awake in that class the entire seven weeks school had been in session. *What'dju expect, Squirt?* He asked himself.

One kid shouted, "Hey, what's the difference between a bitch and a slut?"

Groans came up like another haze of steam. "Old one, Harris!"

This didn't stop the kid named Harris. "A slut sleeps with everybody, but a bitch sleeps with everybody but *you*."

"Nice!" someone called sarcastically.

"Christ that's ancient," another said.

"You're a regular king among men, Harris," someone else added.

The smell of stinky socks and sweaty under-

Douglas Clegg

arms was all-encompassing, as much of a visible cloud as the steam; the locker room was the one place where shouting and rowdy behavior were tolerated, and the tribe of boys there took full advantage of it; although the cries and booming voice of Bilge as he and Coach went at each other seemed to rise above it all.

Jim reached for his button-down shirt, when one of the scrawny seventh graders passed through the gauntlet of torment, and began crying when he couldn't find his locker again.

The kid could barely keep his towel up, and he looked about as scrawny as a grasshopper as he hopped around. His hair was a little too long. Not quite the Harrow regulation cut, but sometimes the new kids got away with it until Old Man Chambers came around with his tape measure and scissors, saying, "Only a half inch over the ears, young men, half inch, that's all, otherwise, I cut."

"Maybe it's that one over there," Jim said. He pointed to the one in the corner, its door open, a small knapsack sticking out of it.

"Yes," the boy said formally. "That's it."

He went to dress; Jim slipped into his briefs and khakis, buckling his belt too rapidly—too tight, so he let it out slightly. He grabbed his tie from the hook in his locker and tossed it around his neck, then twisted it around his collar. His socks were nowhere to be found, and one of his shoes was missing. This was not unusual for post-gym tragedy—the boys often stole each other's things and hid them somewhere in the labyrinth of the lockers.

He went looking for the missing items. The seventh grader, all dressed in a flash, followed him like a puppy.

"It's mean the way they are," the younger boy said.

Someone on the other side of the locker shouted, "Man, who farted? Warner, you fart? You let out a boomer, Warner? Whew, something died in here, damn!"

"Mean for hiding my shoe?" Jim said. "Ah-ha, watch! I can outsmart them every single time." He withdrew the lost oxford from atop a tall locker. "They throw them, but never too far." He retrieved his socks, which hung from one of the overhead lights. "Here ya go. See? Nothing's hidden very long in this place."

As he laced up, the boy watched him carefully.

"You're new here," the boy said.

"Not that new," Jim said. "I was here half of last year."

"I guess I'm the new one, huh?" the boy giggled. "You seem new here anyway."

"I'm not a lifer. I didn't go to Hope or Parham before here, like most of you guys. I was in public school before. In Bronxville." He added this last bit of background as an afterthought. He cringed; it felt like a lie. It felt like he was trying to make out that he'd gone to a good public school in a rich neighborhood. Well, he had. Until he was eleven. Then he'd just gone to a regular old public school in a regular old neighborhood.

"It's like prison here," the boy said. Then he thrust his hand out. "Miles."

"Miles, good to meet you. You're in East?"

"Hell," Miles said.

"It'll be over."

"I can't wait to get older," Miles sighed. "I hate East. West looks so key. It really looks key."

"It's not all that key. It's more like lock," Jim laughed. "I'm Jim Hook."

"I knew that. You don't remember, but one time, I saw you in study hall. I have one study hall in West. You brought a note to Farquar. About the fire drill."

"I guess I did," Jim agreed.

"He introduced you to everybody. I sat in the back. I always sit in the back, where no one can see me. If they can't see me they can't bother me."

"Did you get rat-tailed by Shrike?"

"I'm fast. I ran past him." Miles glanced back in the direction of the shower stalls. "Shreve's a bully. They call him Shrike because it's a bird that kills other birds. Someday a hawk will come down and kill the Shrike."

"Sure, or rat-tail his butt till it's red like the

Japanese flag," Jim said. "You got a nickname here, Miles?"

"Why?"

" 'Cause nearly everyone does."

"Do you?"

Jim shrugged. "Not yet. I guess they're unavoidable. I'll call you Mole."

"Mole?"

"Yep. Mole. Like the rodent."

"Okay," Miles grinned. "I guess I can be a rat."

"They're not rats," Jim said. "You never read *Wind in the Willows?*"

Miles shrugged.

"Come on, every kid reads it. In like third grade?"

Miles shook his head. "I never was much for reading that sort of thing," he said, with such a mature air that Jim had to grin. The rich kids at school always seemed preternaturally mature—it was what the moneyed background seemed to do. Jim resented it only slightly; he was hoping to join their ranks someday in the future. He had it all planned out.

"I remember every book I ever read," Jim said. "My first one was called *Goodnight, Moon*. Then one of my favorites when I was your age was *Huckleberry Finn*."

"We have to read this really boring book called *The Red Pony*."

"Steinbeck," Jim nodded. "I never loved that one either." Jim got off the bench and grabbed his notebooks. "Well, hasta la vista, Mole."

"Later, Hook," Miles said.

Jim Hook glanced back at the boy, who watched him just the way Jim had watched his older brother as he went off to high school.

It was a different world, with a huge gulf between the two places: high school and middle school. But at Harrow, the schools all ran together.

"East meets West in the halls of Harrow," old man Chambers would say.

3

In the hallway, Michael-the-Good practically slugged him with his blue knapsack.

"Jim, d'ju study? Your tie is on backward. Here." He began fiddling with the tie that dangled like a loose wire from Jim's neck. "Cripes, *I* sure did, just about all night going over the damn Western Civ, like I give a flyer. Tippy, what's that in your hair? Christ, is that jizz?"

Reginald "Tippy" Tipton had his navy blue blazer pulled tight over his chunky form. He looked like a chipmunk with greasy blond hair; he always seemed a little too high—Jim had heard that Tipton kept vodka in his locker. "It's gel. Shut up," Tippy said.

"Tipton came on hisself, Christ, Jim, did you see that? Tippy came on hisself."

"No I didn't. It's just gel. My hair was all over the place this morning. I barely slept. And Hook here didn't study one bit. I saw you sneak in after lights out. It musta been two A.M."

"Whiners," Alan Tarcher said, passing by, a blur of a boy.

"You didn't study?" Michael-the-Good gasped. "Kelleher's a piece of work. His midterm is notorious."

"It's killer."

"He murders boys with his midterms," Tippy snickered. "Legends. Legacies. They get booted. You flunk Kelleher, you flunk Harrow. He's a ball-buster. He busts your balls so hard they smack back into your ass and then bounce up to your mouth and you spit 'em out."

"That's gross," Jim said, but laughed.

"Hey Mikey, why's your pants got go all those black threads?" Tippy asked, pointing at Michael-the-Good's crotch. "Looks like you're sewing your dick up."

"It's so big I hadda sew it up," Michael-the-Good said, and laughed at his own joke.

"I'm gonna flunk Western Civ. I know it," Jim said.

"Fug it, Jim," Michael-the-Good whispered out of the side of his mouth; Michael-the-Good could never say anything worse than "fug" or "shid" or "clocksucker." It almost seemed nastier that way. "Just play sick. If you have the flu, you can't take the midterm. Cripes, you're an

101

SS, what the hell were you doing last night? We were all cramming till one."

"I was doing something else," Jim said, and glanced at his books, wondering how he'd ever get through his sophomore year.

"Ten minutes to fourth period, and you are screwed, Hook, screwed by the king himself, King Kelleher, all hail King Stinky." Tippy's voice echoed along the breezeway as he began running to get to class. The buzzer was going off, and that meant that Jim Hook had less than nine minutes to learn as much as he could about the Albigensian Heresy and the Cathars and perhaps even the fall of Jerusalem before the dreaded midterm from the ball-buster Kelleher.

He knew what was at stake.

4

"Someone stole the keys," Old Man Chambers announced, his voice echoing through the breezeway, the boys scattering like pigeons as his voice assaulted them—asthmatic and wheezy and too much like the breath of the dead to their young ears.

"Someone stole the keys and someone will pay for it," he added, raising his fist as if to strike down in some biblically epic way the perpetrator of this dark and nefarious crime. "Someone stole the keys to the stacks in the library, and now we need to call a locksmith, you thieves of literature! All the old books are there, all the special editions this school has amassed, and one of you or many of you are out to plunder that treasure!"

Students who hadn't flown like birds from his voice shrugged him off as they hurried to classes or walked swiftly toward study halls or morning duties or the library to study in the last hour before some dreaded midterm exam.

And still Chambers ranted, his figure becoming more Moses-like as he railed, as he pronounced the great commandment of "Thou Shalt Not Take the Keys!"

It wasn't that unusual for the 'Row—Chambers's keys often went a-missing, and then some prank would be played on him, or the keys would turn up again in his raincoat's pocket or hanging from St. George's horse's ear out at the fountain.

5

Jim tossed his books on the leather couch near the entrance to the library, and plopped down. The couch let out a big fart sound, but he ignored the snickers that emanated from down by the reading tables near the displays and magazine racks.

Scarecrow MacDrinnan came by and asked something, but Jim was too worried about

Western Civ and blew him off. He opened the *Ages of Civilization* book, and flipped through the pages, trying to focus on some subject related to the Crusades or the Inquisition, but none of it seemed to add up to anything.

Everything was about Popes and schisms and which was the damn crusade that had the children, or one crusade that someone named Peter the Hermit began, and it all meant nothing to him even though he had sat in class for weeks, every day in Western Civ. For some reason that was the one subject that made no sense to him. And Kelleher's lectures—it was like hearing a lullaby after being awake for three days. Snoozeville.

For a split second, he wondered if perhaps it was the Hundred Years' War and Joan of Arc and the Dauphin he was supposed to have been following—those were things that somehow stuck out in his mind.

He had given a presentation with Michael-the-Good on the Golden Age of Athens the third week of the term, and then it seemed as if they'd gone from there right up to the Knights Templar and the Saracens, although he might've mixed it up too much in his head. Something about Saladin and something about Richard the Lion-Hearted and maybe even the Magna Carta was in there, although he might've gotten that screwed up. And the dates? Holy shit, what were the dates?

And why the hell was this the one class he never could get? He was doing fine in English and okay in Latin and semigood in Spanish, and Math was never better than a C but you can't have everything and he never flunked that kind of stuff, but this history class for some reason was the most boring course he had ever taken, and maybe it was the teacher. Yeah, it had to be.

Either that, or you're just stupid, he told himself. Smart kids don't even need to study. They get through this stuff. Stephen aced everything here. Stephen had loved Kelleher, and Kelleher had apparently never forgotten Stephen Hook, because every chance he could, Kelleher reminded Jim that he was not like his brother, that Stephen was always on top of Western Civ, and if only, Kelleher had added, all students were as bright and charming as Stephen Hook had been. . . .

And for some reason, Jim could not live up to any of it in that class because there was something about Kelleher himself that made Jim tune out, that got him thinking about anything but Western Civ, that got him daydreaming or wondering about an upcoming class or making a mental list of the errands he needed to run on the weekend or how much laundry he needed to drop off at the service in town.

It was almost as if the more Kelleher talked about how Stephen had been this shining paragon of studious ability and brilliance, the more likely it was that Jim would begin to blank on anything that went on in class. And it never ended in class: the Western Civ book looked like a bunch of words and dates put together that didn't add up to anything intelligible.

Or, you're just stupid, Jim thought. *You need to apply yourself. You need to rise to the challenge.*

All that bullshit.

6

He glanced up at the clock above the reference shelf. He had three minutes to make up for several weeks' worth of studies that he hadn't quite kept up with.

I'm screwed.

"Yo Hook."

Jim glanced up. "Yo Fricker."

Trey Fricker the Third stood there, still sweating from cross-country practice. The sweat poured through his white shirt; his tie was slightly askew. The other kids called Fricker "Brad" for Brad Pitt, even though Fricker looked harsher and sometimes even a little handsomer than any movie star could, but sometimes Jim could tell Fricker liked being nicknamed for a handsome actor rather than the horrible things most of the kids got their names from (like Bilge, Shrike, and Shitfor-

brains Turner, who never lived that one down).
"You not ready?"

"I die today," Jim said.

"You went to see Lark?"

"Yeah," Jim said. "She's doing good. And to-day . . . I fail a midterm."

"Naw, it's cake. Don't worry, it's cake. It's the cakest test in all Christendom." Fricker said crap like that all the time. *This is the best meat-loaf in all Christendom. Man, she's built like the briskest shit-house in all Christendom*. It cracked everyone up, and it was practically his trade-mark.

"I hear it's gonna be a nightmare."

"That's Michael-the-Good talk," Fricker said. "Did you see the way Michael-the-Good's pants were sewn up? Man, it looks vaginal. All these threads. It was freaky. He should just buy a new pair of pants, Kee-rist. Your pants split in the crotch, buy yourself a new pair, that's what I say."

Trey Fricker was the only guy in his class that Jim had known before passing all the entrance exams and getting the scholarships to Harrow— Fricker's dad had known Jim's dad, and Fricker's brother had been in Stephen's class three years earlier.

Fricker was half the reason Jim had agreed to pursue going to Harrow at all. Fricker had an easy way about him. Jim felt as if he were around some kind of celebrity with Fricker, whose dad, though divorced from his mother, played for the Baltimore Orioles and made millions. Fricker's mom was some big publishing executive.

Fricker seemed to maneuver in and out of the social groups both in school and out of it—he knew all the girls at St. Anne's and St. Cat's and the Robbins School. He drove a Mercury Cougar that was nearly brand-new.

He was a nice guy, someone who seemed to see through all the bullshit and shallowness of some of the more popular guys in school. Fricker, in fact, had pretty much looked out for Jim, and Jim felt in debt to him from the word go. Fricker had what Jim thought of as "star quality," some kind of aura of excitement and interest and basic knowledge of the working parts of life.

"Look," Fricker said. "I'll give you the rundown on this. First, Kelleher always tips his hand."

"What do you mean?"

"I mean," Fricker laughed, "he can't help trying to show how smart he is. So what you need to do is scan the whole test first to see if he answers an early question later on. He always does."

"What about the essay questions?"

"Bullshit. Make up some bullshit. You can do that, Hook, I've heard you do it enough in English."

"Yeah, but the Crusades . . ."

"Here's all you need to know about the Crusades," Fricker said, and pulled him off the couch, practically dragging him down the hall to Room 23, regaling him with what Fricker called "the Six Salient Points of the Holy Crusades."

Chapter Ten
The Test

1

No teacher at the high school level is without some oddity, some eccentricity, some mannerism that can be exploited and lampooned by any number of talented students.

Kelleher was a praying mantis of a man.

He was both self-satisfied and voracious. He was a dark and disturbed soul.

He was reed-thin, his hair longish, which seemed radical for the conservative school, and his clothes ill-suited for his frame—he also generally smelled, which led to his nickname: Stinky.

He could not have been more than forty, yet

something about him already seemed wizened and ancient. His blackboard was scuffed with old chalk diagrams that had been erased and then layered upon by other diagrams and then erased again until it was like the dust of bones.

A huge, tattered map of Western Europe covered one wall, and on another, a map of the pre-Columbian Americas. His desk was piled with papers that he had left ungraded, and whenever a student asked for one of these back, Kelleher would tell him that his was the one failing grade, but Kelleher was considering revising his opinion. Usually, the student never asked for his paper twice.

He always kept the shades drawn in his classroom, and he had a sniggering way of speaking.

Kelleher was, in a word, repulsive.

Particularly to boys of fifteen, all of whom would rather be anywhere but sitting there, looking up at him with his pile of little blue books.

"All books, beneath your desks," Kelleher began. "All that should be on top of your desks are two number 2 pencils and one large eraser. The midterm will take you approximately one hour and ten minutes. That ten minutes will cut into some of your lunch periods. For others, it will cut into your study halls. I do not give a damn where your ten minutes come from. You are not to leave this room until ten minutes after the hour. Each of you will receive one of these." He held up a blue book. "There are fifteen pages in each one. I expect you to fill them all."

The groan rose like a muted chorus from the fourteen students in the class.

"Every page should be filled. Within each blue book, you will find your midterm. There are approximately thirty-five true or false questions on this midterm, each worth two points. Then, there are two essay questions. Each essay question is worth fifteen points. Should you fail to attempt to answer any question, that will count double the points against you. As you know, term is up in five weeks, when the Christmas vacation begins. Should any of you fail this exam, it would be advisable that you prepare yourself for a failing grade for the term unless you have a way of coming back on the final with a score of one hundred percent."

"Sir?" Walter Allen asked from the back row.

"Allen?"

"What's passing, sir?"

Kelleher sighed, rolling his eyes. "The same as for any other test, Mr. Allen. Seventy is passing, anything below seventy is failure."

"But a sixty-eight isn't failing. It's a D," Allen said.

"Mr. Allen." Kelleher began walking over to his desk, then stopped midaisle. "You have just lost five points from your midterm for saying something asinine. Now, when I say pencils down, I mean pencils down. When the test is over, you will write what, Mr. Howard?"

"The Pledge."

"And tell me what that pledge is, Mr. Howard?"

"I pledge that I have not lied, cheated, or stolen with regards to this exam or any activity at Harrow Academy, and duly acknowledge this with my signature," Ross Howard said. Then he quickly added, "And then we sign our names."

"Good, Mr. Howard. Now, are you ready to meet your dooms, boys?"

Some of the boys laughed, but Jim kept his head down. He looked at the graffiti on his desk ("Kelleher's a dick"; "Cadavers"; "Tell Laura I love her"). Then he glanced sidelong at Fricker, who sat to his right.

Fricker caught his look, nodding slowly.

After the blue books and the test were passed out, Kelleher said, "Now, class, open your midterms." Then he went back to sit behind his desk.

Jim looked down at the test before him.

All right, true and false you can figure out. Remember what Fricker told you. He practically answers his own questions somewhere in here.

The first ten or so questions were pretty much common sense, and Jim remembered some things from class, and a little from some of the reading he had done a couple of weeks before. Others, he hazarded what he considered decent guesses. Something caught his eye—it was

Fricker twiddling his pencil beneath his desk.

Jim looked over to him.

Trey Fricker had pushed his blue book a little bit farther to the left. Jim could practically see all his answers. Trey nodded slightly, barely giving Jim a look. He mouthed the word: *okay*.

Jim looked up at the clock. Forty-five minutes left. He scanned the room. All heads were down—they were all concentrating on the exam. Kelleher leaned back in his chair, reading. Jim looked back at Fricker's blue book. Fricker had set the exam as close to the edge of his desk as it could get without falling. He had placed a check mark beside each true or false.

Jim looked back at his paper.

He wasn't a cheater.

If I fail, I fail.

He looked at his first few true/false answers. Then, over to Fricker's checkmarks. Fricker, who knew this subject backward and forward, had completely opposite answers.

Jim felt his pulse race. This midterm was nothing. It was just a midterm. Sure he was SS—and being a Scholarship Student came with its own set of pressures. He had to keep his average in each subject above a 3.0, and if it looked like he was failing, he could easily lose the fourteen-thousand-a-year scholarship payment that it took to stay at Harrow.

He had already begun slipping, well before this test, and he knew that he had been sleep-

walking through Western Civ for the better part
of the term. He just had not been keeping up,
and his mind wandered whenever Kelleher gave
his digressive lectures. His class notes were gib-
berish and doodles—he could not keep his
mind alert in this one class.

He knew what would happen if he failed.

He felt a trickle of sweat along his back.
Something like fingers pressing down beneath
his skull.

*Don't psych yourself out. You won't lose every-
thing because of some dumb test.*

Some dumb midterm.

*Why didn't you study? Why did you let seeing
Lark get in the way of it? Why are you worried
now when you should've been worried last
month when you weren't even cracking the book?
And when you did finally open the Western Civilization book, the words looked like a foreign language to you, and all you could think about was
how your mom was going to feel if you did badly
here, how she was depending on you. How you
need to get the best education and go to the best
college and get a top job so you can support her
so she'll never have to be humiliated again—not
the way she was humiliated by her family and
your father's family, and the bank and the collection agency . . .*

*And you wanted to show these rich snobs a
thing or two.*

You were going to show them, weren't you?

Weren't you?

Not just failing a class. This would be failing both his father and his brother, both of whom could no longer "make good" as his grandmother would say about people. Jim and his mother had once been upper middle class, but that was before his father died, and with him, the means for making good money.

Jim's mother, who was generally sad and in need of a daily dose of what Jim had come to call "emergency wine," had trouble bringing in enough to pay for even his school ties.

So, Jim worked in the summer, and would soon begin to do afternoons in the headmaster's office, filing papers and typing (a useful skill which he'd taught himself at the age of nine because he wanted to write stories for his brother, who had always taken pride in them). He and his mother were nearly poor, and this scholarship was the only dream his mother seemed to have left. He did not intend to lose it.

Intend being the operative word.

The road to failure, he had once heard his father say about a friend of his parents, is paved with good intentions.

And Jim was screwing it up big time.

He could feel the screwup coming like the lightning flash of inevitability that struck him occasionally when he knew something was about to go wrong. It didn't always go wrong. But it usually felt like it should.

His head pounded. He'd had headaches since the day his brother had died, not every day, just certain days, certain moments, when he was thinking about things too much.

And now, it came on full force.

The Queen Mother Bitch of all headaches.

For just a second, he thought he heard something. It was in his mind, he knew.

He could practically hear his grandmother's voice:

"You're going to go crazy like your sister," she said, and although she had said it to his mom, it felt as if it had been said to him, too. "You're going to start hearing things and seeing things and pretty soon, you'll just be in that yellow room with nurses, and someone will have to pay. Someone always has to pay, don't they, for people like you?"

Jim was sure he heard something—some wild animal—scratching at a door, not just any door, but an attic door, and it was the night of his brother's death, and he wore his dinosaur pajamas and he felt very brave and went to the foot of the stairs to the attic and watched the door—

Something's coming through.

2

It had been a dream, he was sure.

But the sound was in his head now.

The scratching. The door within his mind's eye was growing—it was moving toward him, and he was moving toward it.

Something's coming through, Jimmy.

Here it comes.

Here it comes.

The voice of a woman whispered: Watch out for the Rat Changer.

He opened his eyes again to the classroom. His body was soaked in sweat. For just a second, he thought he saw—

But he knew his eyes were not focusing—

The map behind Kelleher's desk shimmered like a pond that's been disturbed by a fish—

He shot a glance at Fricker's paper.

He changed his trues to falses and falses to trues. Fricker angled the blue book pages so he could get a better look. His Ts and Fs were huge.

Then, Jim got to the first essay question.

Christ, how am I going to copy Fricker's essay?

But there was the question, like a big fat lump of shiny gold, staring him in the face.

The question read: *Name and discuss the Six Salient Points of the Holy Crusades as discussed in the text and in class.*

3

Jim grinned and nearly sighed. He shook his head, feeling relief. God, he was going to pass this. He glanced over at Fricker's paper for a moment.

And that's when someone behind him—was it Carrington?—shouted, "Hey, Hook's cheating!"

Jim looked up and saw Kelleher slowly set down the book he had been reading. Watching him.

Observing.

It was over for him.

This was death.

"How you gonna make your big bro proud?" a voice whispered in his mind.

Chapter Eleven
Dishonor

1

Harrow Academy is most proud of its Honor Code.

No one within its jurisdiction—and this includes all teachers, students, employees, and alumni—should tolerate the taint of dishonor upon the name of Harrow.

It is absolutely required that students turn in their classmates when they are observed violating the Code. The power and beauty of the Code and the faith and belief within the Harrow community of students and faculty depend on each individual's co-operation.

An Honor Code is only as good as the community that supports it. Each student will need to follow their consciences at some time in relation to the Code. It is the obligation of all members of the Harrow community to uphold it, to turn in friend, neighbor, enemy, comrade, and yes, even brother should it come to this, without thought to relationship. Dishonor will never be the light of our school community. We must seek truth, justice, and honor to become men who will lead the world.

It is in the often-unpleasant task of accusation and the subsequent reporting of Honor Code violators that the Code will prevail.

In determining what action to take after witnessing a possible Honor Code violation, one should remember that the Honor Council's main purpose is not to punish students but to sustain an atmosphere of honor in the school and to help individual students understand the meaning of the Code. The best way to ensure that an atmosphere of honor exists is not to tolerate violations of the Honor Code. This may be done in many ways, one of the most effective of which is consulting with a teacher or the headmaster. While it is understood that reporting a friend or peer may be difficult, doing so is most often best for that student and for our community. Clearly, the preservation of the Honor System depends on the willingness of each community member to step forward and not tolerate Honor Code violations.

2

Lying, cheating, stealing.

The three magic words at Harrow for getting the boot.

Jim had been told this when he entered. Dean Angstrom, the Disciplinary Counseler, had told him, "We are most proud of our honor system, which is ironclad here at Harrow." Jim had been sitting with his mother in the man's office the previous winter, a midyear entry into Harrow. On the wall, a large cat-o'-nine-tails was meant as a bit of a joke, Angstrom explained, since he was in charge of discipline.

Jim's hair had just been cut, and he felt squirmy in the blazer and tie, since, in his last school, he'd gotten away with jeans and regular shirts, sometimes even T-shirts.

"Our boys take pride in this system," Angstrom had said. "On every paper, every test, they sign a pledge of their honor. Should a boy violate the honor code, justice is speedy. All it takes is one witness. All it takes is a reasonable suspicion. We do not brook any dishonesty here. While we are lenient in cases where a student has perhaps not understood what his dishonesty has been, we often hold a student council honor trial as soon as possible.

"Then a jury of a student's peers determine if a violation has truly occurred.

"We ring the chapel bells six times when a student is expelled for an honor violation. It is a sad, shameful moment. I'm happy to say this has only happened four times in the past twenty-three years that I've been here.

"Each time, the student in question was in clear violation of the code."

3

Of course, Jim knew a few boys who routinely stole, several more who lied as if their lives depended upon it, and guessed that with one or two, cheating on tests was not the most abnormal pastime.

But he knew, just as well as the next 'Row student, that getting caught was the thing.

And now, he had delivered himself into their hands.

Stupidly.

He looked over at Fricker, who, out of fear, had turned to face forward, his blue book closed.

4

The idea of the Honor Council gave him the creeps, too.

No one knew who they were or what they did. There were legends of boys sent packing in the night for various violations, but the tales were tall ones and too numerous to be accurate. Michael-the-Good was asked to escort Jim back to his dormitory to await the scheduling of the honor trial—and it wasn't even three in the afternoon yet. "I'm screwed," Jim whispered to him as they walked out into the breezeway.

"No talking," Michael-the-Good said. "Sorry, Hook. It's the rules."

"Damn," Jim said. "And double-damn. Shit to hell."

"It's bad to curse," Michael-the-Good added, walking ahead of him like a priest with a man headed for the gas chamber.

5

Walking down West on his way to a class, Old Man Chambers caught him by the scruff of his neck. The old geezer was like a walking corpse, in a black jacket and tie and a rib cage that could be seen right through his starched white shirt, but he was strong like he lifted weights even at eighty. "Boy, I hear you crossed a line,"

Chambers said, his voice half cough and half whisper.

Jim just looked up at him. "Yeah."

"Your father would not like this," Chambers muttered, letting him go. The old man turned and headed back down toward the library, muttering and cursing to himself. Then, briefly, he turned to face Jim again.

"Were you the boy who stole my keys?" Chambers asked.

"Sir?" Jim nearly choked. What new crimes would he be accused of, now that he was marked with dishonor?

"My keys. The master set. They've gone a-missing. Did you take them?" Chambers had a look on his face like he already had suspected as much.

It almost wouldn't matter what Jim said now.

6

At four, Jim had to sit with Dean Angstrom, the man's words buzzing around him like yellow jackets, his face red.

He'd been unable to look the Disciplinary Counseler in the eye. Then he'd gone to his two-hour, twice-a-week job in the school library, reshelving the day's books as part of his work-study program, and even Mrs. Finch wouldn't say a word to him.

Someone had pulled out two books on the occult and left them smack dab in the middle of the magazine racks. One was called, quite simply, *The Occult*, by someone named Colin Wilson, and the other was a raggedly bound book called *The Infinite Ones* by someone with the strangest name Jim had run across in a while (and he noticed all oddly named authors).

The name was Isis Claviger, and he imagined some drawn, wizened old lady of seventy scribbling away. Perhaps it was the terrible day, perhaps it was the fact he hadn't eaten since noon, or perhaps it was because the name, Isis Claviger, sounded either like a cheap French wine or the piss-elegant wife to some custodian, but he began giggling.

The book dropped from his hand—slipped— and when he picked it up, he opened it as he walked over to the shelf where it belonged.

The book was so old that the binding was cracked and sloppily taped, as were some of the pages, which were thin as tissue paper. He glanced through the table of contents: phrases like *lucid somnambulism* and *ectoplasmic manifestations* and *astral fragmentary hives* dotted the chapter headings.

A thin waxy paper covered some frontispiece illustration.

He drew the paper back, and there was a photograph of one of the most beautiful women Jim had ever seen. She had a strong chin, and thick, sensual lips.

She was young when the photograph was taken—he checked the copyright date, which was listed as 1912. Isis Claviger definitely looked like a woman of her time—from the shadows around her eyes to the long curling locks that cascaded around her shoulders. There was something rough and unrefined about her as well; and yet her eyes were compelling and singularly bright compared to the rest of the old photograph. It was almost as if someone had retouched the eyes to clean the whites up, and had also managed to reveal the translucence in the iris. She must've been a hot babe of his great-grandpa's generation.

He chuckled to himself, thinking of it.

She was, as his grandfather had once said of his grandmother, "calamitously beautiful," which, to Jim's mind, meant dazzling. She could've been a silent movie star or something. Something like the winsome actresses in those old movies, almost girlish, almost woman-esque, almost radiant.

Beneath her name, a lengthy and curious phrase, scribbled sloppily—some of the lines crossed over each other in an elaborate and messy hand—in faded blue ink:

Thelma without my bidding what comes with the ankle comes from the lurking of (then, two words that Jim couldn't make out). *All the barns within the ratchanger and the Raise is here with*

his beloved ones I met the one they call the Thou-
sandth One

The rest of the nonsensical phrase had been
rubbed out.

He turned the ragged pages, some with yel-
lowed Scotch tape, some torn at the roots, and
found some more drawings and photographs in
the book. One showed a woman at a small
round table, her hands on the shoulders of two
men on either side of her. Another woman,
more diminutive, stood behind the man with
the glaring eyes.

The caption read:

Isis Claviger with Aleister Crowley, Victor Neu-
burg, and Rose Kelly on the eve of the Anubis
Invocation, Cairo, 1904.

Chapter Twelve
The Book

1

Isis Claviger was startlingly beautiful in this photograph—Jim felt a gasp rising in his throat as he looked at her, because she looked more contemporary than the men sitting beside her; the woman who stood behind them looked as if she were trying to disappear in the shadows. The woman called Isis wore what looked like a tuniclike robe, and Jim was almost convinced he saw her left breast falling out the side—but it didn't look cheap. She looked like a goddess of a woman.

He went and checked the book out, curious that Harrow would even have such a bizarre volume, and then finished reshelving for the day.

He took a few minutes, plopping down on a couch, and leafed through the pages, mainly glancing at the pictures. It took his mind off what lay ahead of him:

The torment of dishonor.

The anxiety of knowing his doom.

A picture of the pyramids of Egypt with two figures wrapped up like sheiks sitting on a camel. A picture of a large man with piercing eyes. Beneath this, the caption: *The Beast, on a not-so-beastly day*.

Another photo was nearly shredded down the middle and then scotch-taped to hell: It was Isis Claviger, the author of the book, holding what looked like a small jewel—it reminded Jim of a stick figure. The caption read, *I. C. with her beloved ankh, given to her by Amon Ra in a past incarnation.*

Okay. Whatever the hell an ankh is.

He flipped through the pages, until he saw something quite stunning: a beautiful house that had some disturbance about it—like an aura, only dark, and Jim figured it was some trick of the photographer, for it looked as if the photo were taken during an eclipse, with the darkened sun just over the rooftop. Something about the house was quite beautiful and grand, and he figured it was one of those English manors. All the caption said was, "The Place of the

Seven Dreamers." A man stood before the arched doorway; then Jim noticed that part of the house, toward the back left of it, was still under construction.

He drew the book closer to his eyes. Did he need glasses? There were designs along the various gables of the house—what were they? They looked intricate—gargoyles? Some kind of dragons? And symbols—stars? Moons? It was hard to tell, and the more Jim squinted trying to make out the images, the more they seemed to move.

Hold it in. Keep it in, he thought. He had understood how his imagination got out of control. He sometimes saw things in the dark, or imagined terrors at dawn—he had never expressed this to anyone, but he knew it was not something the students at Harrow Academy needed to know.

It was almost hypnotic, looking at the photograph of the house—because the more he stared at it, the more he began noticing further detail—how the grass was tamped down in circles to the edge of the driveway to the steps; how the glass in the windows was beveled and swirled in its own circular pattern; how each corner, each edge, each doorway and window, seemed to be slightly off-kilter, as if it had been designed to be not quite right.

Then he had to pull back; look away. His head was starting to ache.

What a day.

He flipped through some other photos—pictures of séances, complete with gauzy spirits in the background, some palace in some city called Pescador, and a French château called Barbebleau, and then some monastery somewhere, and there, in the picture, Isis Claviger again, with two men whose faces were blurred by the bad camera work.

Chapters spun by as he got the pages going, and he was about to close the book when he found what at first looked like a piece of tissue paper. He carefully drew the paper out, and saw that it had writing on it. He opened it carefully.

All it said was:

You will find this when you are meant to. We are not gone. We are not free, as was promised. We have been waiting for you to shut the door. Someone must shut the door.

2

An Excerpt from Chapter One of *The Infinite Ones*

All who read this book are already adepts and will understand the secrets contained herein. Should someone who is not part of our understanding approach these words, he will only see the descriptions of travels and séances and spiritual pursuits of both the light and dark variety.

I did not come to this world without an understanding, as I am a Natural. It has been estimated that there are fewer than two thousand of us in the English-speaking world at any one time, although I dispute this figure. I believe there are certain high birth rates throughout history, usually after catastrophic wars, in which the number of Naturals increases. Perhaps this accounts for the heightened interest in the spiritual world at the recent century's end. Perhaps this is what has driven the world to my door, the princes and duchesses and monied of Europe and the United States to hire my services. It was in just such a way that I made the acquaintance of the subject of this book.

Aleister Crowley. Called a Devil by some, a priest by others. He is neither, in my estimation. He is a seeker after Wisdom, and with Wisdom comes great price. So, Crowley has paid the price with his reputation, but in return he has brought things into the world beyond the reach of even the finest conjurers.

I was with him for the Anubis Invocations, as detailed in the series of articles published in *The Occultist* during the winter of 1910, some of which are reprinted here, and more recently traveled with him to Jerusalem and then Chinon for the investigation into the sacred Templar wall writings.

This book was written over a period of three years, as I acted as the medium for Crowley's spiritual guide, and it was during that time that I traveled further along on my inner journey toward illumination in the world beyond this one.

It all began in April one year when I had only just visited the famous murderer in New England whom I shall not name, a woman of refinement who showed me every courtesy. I had a note from an admirer, a man who told me he followed my writings with a fanatic's zeal, and who wanted me to come see something that he believed would so stir my mind and heart that I would lose all interest in table-rappings and anything so base as communication with the dead.

This is the story of my journey to the place in question, of my studies and travels with Aleister Crowley, and my knowledge of the Other Side. . . .

3

After setting the book in his hall locker, Jim went to use the restroom—it was after seven

P.M., and the corridor was empty. He had to walk down the corridor to East for the fastest way to his room, but he dreaded the events to come. The library had taken his mind off of it all for a short time.

The bathroom door seemed locked at first, but when he tried it again, it opened.

The hall lights flickered a firefly yellow, and the restroom itself had dim flickering fluorescents overhead.

The place was empty, and the lights lit the restroom so poorly that it was as if the electric bill hadn't been paid.

When he got into a stall, someone switched the lights off completely.

A couple of guys swung the stall doors open, grabbed him, and pulled him out.

Chapter Thirteen
Captive

1

They threw him against the tile wall.

Jim felt an explosion inside his skin, and was worried that he'd broken something—but the thought was momentary, as he felt their hands pinching at his wrists—

He tried to shout, but the wind had been knocked out of him, and it was all he could do to keep breathing—

He felt his blood pulse within his body like the pounding of surf against a shore—

Beyond the mottled-glass windows of the restroom, the breezeway was lit with round orbs of white light that created shadows in the darkness of the restroom; he saw their dark forms, perhaps four or five of them, but couldn't tell who they were.

One of them gave the lowdown while he caught his breath. "Keep your mouth shut, you'll live. Listen, Hook, if you don't work the system, the system works you. Now, you can stay and suffer under this shit-eating rule that they have, or you can be one of us, join up, pledge allegiance to us. Once that happens, you'll be a prince among men, and you don't need to worry your sorry ass about any of this bullshit. Now, Hook, you in, you out? You ready to bend over while they ram a log as big as a redwood up your butt, or do you become superior and work the system? 'Cause when we choose to recruit somebody, we don't candyass it, we need to know a yes or a no, and if it's a no, I'm sorry to say, we're going to be the ones who make your life more miserable than even those sons of bitches could ever dream of doing."

He heard his own panting breaths, there in the dark, and it sounded like fear. How many were there? Who were they? How could he make this kind of decision given the massacre he was going to face the following morning?

Jim Hook stood there for a minute, thinking about how his life had changed so quickly, with a momentary and stupid decision.

"Who *are* you?" he asked the shadows.

"Your worst nightmare," one of them answered. "Or your saviors. It's up to you."

2

"You don't know who we are. Not yet. And you're not going to. Not until we know for sure you're with us. All you really need to know is that we know who you are. We know things about you that you don't even know," one of them said, and the voice was achingly familiar, but Jim couldn't place it.

Was it Falmouth? Falmouth was a senior from the Midwest. Maybe it was Falmouth. Maybe Falmouth and . . . Captain Joe?

No, not Captain Joe, the other voice that spoke must've been Alan McComber, another senior.

Had to be.

Before he could respond, something slapped over his eyes, and then he smelled something that reminded him of pine needles and cedar, and before he had very nearly figured out one of the shadow's voices, he felt his stomach lurch, and his knees felt like jelly, and he tried to reach for something to steady himself. The dizziness was fast, and he thought if he just held on for another second or two, he could fight them, fight them and get out of this.

As if the world had sliced off from his mind,

141

he stood, a little boy, in front of the attic door and listened to them scratching.

3

Something's coming through.

The scratching grew louder, and then he heard what sounded like a chainsaw grinding.

All doors were meant to be open.

The doorknob was rattling, and a chainsaw was on the other side of the door with the wild animal. It was beginning to cut through the wood.

All secrets were meant to be told.

The door began to bulge outward, wood splinters flying as the chainsaw cut through, as the doorknob rattled—

Jim began moving toward the door to get closer to what was there, on the other side.

Something's coming through.

4

When he awoke, he wasn't sure if he was dreaming or if in fact he was bound with rope in a room that was so pitch black he didn't even know for sure if his eyes were open or not. Something—some cloth—had been drawn tight across his lips, hurting him slightly. Breathing was difficult until he realized that he could breathe through his nose without a problem. He began to panic, and he tried to regulate his breathing so that he'd calm down.

Whatever was happening was not as bad as it seemed. He remembered how his brother would always tell him that. Eighty percent of what you're afraid will come to pass won't happen, his brother used to tell him. It's that twenty percent you have to watch out for.

This was the twenty percent.

No one is going to kill you. They're probably not going to hurt you.

They're just guys like you.

They're messed up, but they're just guys.

5

In the dark:

"All right, Hook, here's the deal. You came to Harrow late, basically. You're at a serious disadvantage here," one invisible boy said.

Another added, "We've followed you since you came. We know all kinds of things about you."

It was chilly in the dark room. He smelled something like mold. Dampness as well. It was somehow wet where they were. Cold and wet. Another smell—body odor. Someone hadn't washed in a long time.

Jim moved his hands, which were tied in front of him. The rope that bound him was somehow connected to the one that bound his

143

ankles; and somehow this was connected to the rope around his waist. He was hog-tied. He was in the grip of something worse than ropes. He was sure. This was something twisted. These were—no doubt—the real psychopaths of school, the kids who stepped on baby birds and probably were capable of just about anything.

6

"Don't struggle. It makes the ropes go tighter. Trust us. It does. Don't. Don't struggle. Now, Hook, just relax. The ropes are tied in the Magus knot. It can only get tighter when you move. Stay still. No one is going to hurt you."

"We've seen your file. Got it from Chambers's files. We know you're in a spot with this Honor Trial. Here's what happens with an Honor Trial, when you go before them. All it takes is one person to claim they saw you cheating. One person. You already know that Kelleher may not be that person. But his word carries weight. And another student brought the charge. We can fix things so that you will be in no danger of expulsion."

"That's right," someone said, so close to his ear it was like a buzzing fly.

Why couldn't he figure out who they were? In his mind he tried to imagine the yearbook photos of the upperclassmen, and he couldn't match the voices to any of them.

Mischief

"Let me tell you something about your mother that you don't even know. Do you know how much she has to survive on each month? We know."

You couldn't know that! Jim wanted to shout, but the strap over his lips pinched his jaw. Profanity burst within his skull. He wanted to just shut them up. *Enough!*

"She takes home exactly one thousand two hundred and fifty dollars a month. The rent on the apartment is eight hundred fifty. That leaves her with four hundred dollars a month for food, heat, and telephone, to say nothing of her daily bus fare. Were you aware that when she sends you money—which she does at times—that those weeks she often goes without some meals to make sure you have the odd twenty-dollar bill? She literally goes without food. We know. We check into this kind of stuff when we're considering someone as an initiate. We've gone to Yonkers. We went through the trash to find the bank statements. Yeah. All that stuff. We hear stuff sometimes. On the phone, through friends, maybe the woman who works near her might've said something to someone about how she goes without food on days when she sends money to her brat son who never calls her enough but needs money all the time. Sure, she doesn't tell you, Hook, because then you wouldn't take it, right ? Because despite the fact that you're up for an honor violation, you ac-

145

tually have honor, don't you? You wouldn't dare
take that money if you thought she wasn't eating. You believe her when she tells you there's
plenty. Truth is, when your father died, he left
nothing. There were no savings. He didn't make
all that much for Bronxville—maybe two hundred thousand a year. He was waiting for his
inheritance to be really rich, but you know that
grandmother of yours believes in picking and
choosing what to do with her millions. She
wasn't about to give it to the son who had married below his station. The house and lifestyle
in Bronxville sucked up his money, and then
Stephen's tuition and board took the rest. Your
grandmother is rich, but she won't help your
mother. She hates your mother. You know that,
too. Face it, Hook, you pretend you're as well
off as anyone here, but truth is, you're a poor
boy who's just getting by."

"We know all this because we make it our
business to know everything about the students
here."

"Yes, that's right, Hook. We do."

"Your grandmother hates your mother with
a burning passion. She blames your mother for
the death of your father and one of her grand-
sons. We know this isn't true. We know all of
this."

"All about you," said one of the boys in the
dark.

"Quiet," someone whispered. That voice was

too familiar. He had heard that voice many times. The voice that whispered, "Quiet." *Who was it? Damn, think. Think of everyone. Think of anyone. Bilge? Shrike? Fricker? French? Hardass? Bleeder? Mojo?*

"Your grandmother is a very wealthy woman. She could make your mother's and your life very easy if she wanted to, but she's a selfish, embittered old bitch, and she wants to punish your mother for having taken her son from her. She thinks your mother married for money. So she sends along a pittance—a few hundred dollars a month—to make sure you can wear those buttondown shirts and Dockers and have the occasional new down vest. She also ensured that you would have a scholarship here. It isn't hard to pull those kinds of strings in this sort of institution."

"The night your brother died."

"And your father," someone corrected, his voice getting closer. "That night."

"That night was the beginning of your life, only you probably don't believe it. If you had fallen into the clutches of your grandmother the way your father and Stephen had, you probably would be dead, too. Or you would be turning into the kind of man this institution breeds. We are not about that."

"No. We are about beating this system. We are about rising above it. We are about making it work for each of us rather than working for *it*."

"We are here to make sure the school doesn't eat you alive, Hook. Your grandmother would be happy if you never graduated from Harrow. Your grandmother wants to watch you and your mother suffer."

"We can make sure that you do not get kicked out of Harrow tomorrow at the honor trial. We can make sure that you are exonerated of this grievous and awful charge. The only people who get caught for cheating, Hook, are those that someone is out to get. What you must discover is: Who is out to get you? And why? That is your task. When you have discovered that, then we will bring whatever prejudice we have to bear upon that individual in retribution for this crime. And you, Hook, will understand a meaning of brotherhood which you have not felt since the last day you saw your own brother."

"We are your family here at Harrow. And when you move beyond Harrow, we will still be your family."

"We have brothers from our tribe who have gone on to university and the world outside, but they have always remained in touch. A network, if you will."

"They help us. They help each other. They investigate for us, and we for them. This moment of your midterm exam is fortuitous. We knew you would be in a situation to require our services; and we were hoping that someone as resourceful and intelligent as yourself would be in a position to want to contribute to our group."

"Our club."

"Our fraternity."

"Our society."

"I can almost hear the wheels turning in your head as you lie there, Hook. You are thinking how to undo the ropes. Impossible, I assure you. You are wondering who you will tell when you are finally released. Also impossible, as you will soon discover. You may in fact be trying to figure out a suitable revenge for the students who learned everything about your background and family, who have even learned things—regarding taxes and estates and inheritances—that you do not yet know, and you may never know, about your family. But, as the school motto says, just wait for what will come."

"Is it not true that your father graduated from Harrow in 1975? Is it not also true that your brother, Stephen, was meant to graduate in the spring of 1995? Have you heard the rumors about what your father and brother were doing the night of their deaths in the presumed accident?"

Jim thought he heard someone laugh, but it might've been the other noise—the sound he hadn't noticed at first. It was a fan, whirring. To block out any noise outside whatever room they were in. Whatever dark room this was. They had a fan—no, two electric fans going. Where were they? What room in Harrow could this be? It couldn't be a classroom. An office? Angstrom's office? No. He felt his mind like wild monkeys in a jungle screaming at him to get out, to breathe, to somehow survive this and gain superhuman strength, to break free from whatever held him. But the more he struggled, the tighter the ropes became.

Where the hell had they taken him? Was this the library? Had they somehow gotten some keys to—

Yes, that had to be it!

Old Man Chambers had been going up and down the hall talking about his keys. Someone had stolen them. Stolen them and hadn't given them back.

That's what had happened. These students had stolen the keys and had some room. Chambers's office?

"We will tell you the rumors. They are not pleasant. It was said that your father and brother had gone to some whore in the city. After that they had spent the evening celebrating, drinking at a watering hole called the Blue Glass. Your father, it was reported, drank several martinis, and your brother had shots of whiskey. There is more about the Blue Glass and its customers. Some day we may let you see the report."

"Once you've reached level three."

"A word to the wise, Hook: if you find something that seems unusual, keep it to yourself. It's from us. A small gift."

"Yes. Level three. The Blue Glass is not the sort of place where Harrow graduates are usually found, but something had happened with your brother that year. He was troubled over something. He had stolen something from us. Yes, from us. He knew about us, and he purposefully stole this item. And your father—well, although you couldn't have known this, had a woman in the city."

"Ivy Martin," a deep voice said. Christ, they all sounded alike. "Not a suitable companion, but the kind your father generally enjoyed. She ran a certain business near the meat-packing district of the city, and it was to that place that your brother Stephen and your father went next."

"Let's take a second so it can sink in. It's a lot for him to process."

Jim tried not to conjure up the images their words brought into his mind. He tried not to see his father making love to some woman in a room made of blue glass. For some reason, he imagined blue glass beads hanging in a doorway, and a woman naked from the waist up, standing there, a bottle in her hand. He tried not to see his brother's leering, drunken face, as he drew the snow-white panties off a woman named Ivy Martin whose face was devoid of features.

He felt the wetness of tears in his eyes.

"All right. Look, Hook. You probably do not believe any of this. All we ask is that you allow that this may be rumor, or may be a distortion of facts that were quite different than what was said and reported from that winter night. You see, we do know that Ivy Martin knows more about this. We know this for a fact."

"Why are we telling you all this, Hook? Well, there's a good reason. Right now, you're at level one. This is the level of Trust. We need to know that we can trust you. And you need to know that you can trust us. So your first assignment, to be completed within the three days between now and your Honor Trial, is to find Ivy Martin and confront her. And bring back what she now possesses that your brother stole from us."

Jim wanted to protest: *The Honor Trial is tomorrow! I don't have three days! What the hell did Stephen steal? He wouldn't steal anything, I know he wouldn't! He never stole, he never liked even borrowing things from people. Was Stephen part of this bullshit? What the hell's happening? Someone get me out of here!*

"Confrontation is the first rule."

"Yes, face everything. That is one of our mottos."

"It's very much who we are. There are other issues, too. You'll come to know each one leading up to your initiation."

"We are the ones who make things work in the fucked-up world of Harrow."

"We are the ones who do what needs to be done behind the scenes."

"We stand up for each other and for all of us together."

"We follow a creed. It's a creed you'll learn when you're one of us."

"Our fire will be part of your light."

"We are one hand. A hand needs all its fingers."

"As a body needs all its organs."

"As a mind needs all its understanding."

"As a soul hungers for understanding of the world behind the one we see."

"We survive in absolute secrecy. Mention one thing about us, to anyone, and you will live to regret it. We are all around you. You will not know who we are."

"We are not above the law," someone whispered. "We *are* the law."

Then someone's smelly hand came over his nose, and he struggled against it, but the ropes around him tightened. He couldn't breathe through his mouth. He felt a smack at the back of his head.

Then another.

And another.

They were going to beat him up.

Maybe they were going to kill him.

No!

He struggled against the blows, and then felt a kick in his ribs.

Somebody help me! Christ, somebody help me! Somebody! Anybody!

Then Jim lost consciousness.

Chapter Fourteen
Jim Dreams of a Voice

Something's coming through.

How you gonna make your big bro proud?

Something's coming through.

You're in a room, Jim, a room in your mind, and you're safe here, even though you can hear them scratching at the door. You're safe here. There are things out there that want to get in where you are, but you're not going to let 'em in, are you? You're going to stay in that room and you're going to hear some screams and you're going to hear that scratching at the door, but you're not going to let 'em in, because this is your place, your hideout.

This may even be your own personal asylum, Jim, with pads on the walls, and warm fuzzies to keep you comfortable, but there's always something there, always something scratching at the door.

Don't see what you don't want to see, Jim, you don't have to see what's coming through.

But it's coming for you anyway.

And Jim, it wants to grind your bones to make its bread.

PART TWO
PUNISHMENT

Jack hid beneath the great table, and listened as the Ogre tromped in to the great kitchen. "Fee Fie Foe Fum, I smell the blood of an Englishman. Be he alive or be he dead, I'll grind his bones to make my bread," the creature roared, and though it made Jack shiver, he thought that if the harp's music could soothe the Ogre to sleep, he might just be able to steal the treasure and the magic harp, and return home safely.

The harp's music was high and sweet, an exquisite lullaby, and soon Jack heard the Ogre drop his head to the table, followed by a great snoring.

Jack thought so much about his safety that he, like the Ogre, began to drift off to sleep, listening to the harp's gentle and seductive music.

Chapter Fifteen
The Crypt

1

Jim Hook awoke in the graveyard out among the woods, lying between a headstone and footstone.

He was feeling poorly—that was the only way he could describe what had seeped into his blood and bones since the morning. It wasn't precisely rage, it wasn't just anger, it may have been a lot of hurt, but he had an overall sense that the world was hostile, and nothing that had happened that day had improved on that.

He glanced around, paranoid now that he'd be surrounded by cloaked figures or jeering upperclassmen or pretty much anything, now that

Douglas Clegg

he'd been in that dark room with those Invisibles, as he'd come to think of them.

Panic accompanied paranoia; then a weird calm overcame him for a brief second or two. A calm like clear air within his mind, sweeping out all the dust and confusion.

This kind of shit doesn't really happen. There are no secret societies at Harrow Academy. Not like this one. Not one that could beat you up and throw you in a room of darkness and tell you things about your family that you couldn't even find out yourself.

Maybe it's me going nuts.

He had gone nuts once before. It had been brief, but after his brother and father had died, he'd begun seeing things—nothing much—just things that weren't there. Then he'd begun shouting uncontrollably. Then, in a progression which had been bizarre to even his eleven-year-old mind, he'd started to wet himself pretty much anywhere, and sometimes he'd cuss out loud in the most inappropriate ways.

His mom had joked that she'd have to call an exorcist, but it was simply to a child psychiatrist he'd gone—and found out nothing. The doc had attributed it to the trauma of losing his dad and Stephen, but before he dismissed the problem completely, he had taken Jim aside and held tight to his arm. "Now, you don't want to end up in some padded room somewhere, do you, James?"

Of course not, you quack. He wished he could go back in time and say it. Instead he had just shaken his head a little, feeling as if it weren't a psychiatrist with him but God Himself.

"All you have to do is realize something, James," the doc said, so quietly it felt like punishment. "And that is this: Your brother and your father are dead. You loved them. They're gone. You can't bring them back. And you can't be angry at your mother over this. She didn't do it. Sometimes, terrible things happen, James. Sometimes, you just have to hold in the bad words and the urine and the way you feel. That's all that's happening to you. You're not experiencing anything that others won't experience in their lifetimes. So tell yourself that it's over. You need to say goodbye to the hurt and start healing. It's just life."

It was the biggest piece of bullshit he had ever heard up until that point, but, in fact, the peeing in his pants had stopped, and he had no great desire to cuss out loud—at least not until he'd entered high school.

So, you're not nuts, James, he told himself as he lay feeling the stinging pain in his ribs where someone had hit him too hard.

It's just fugged-up life, as Michael-the-Good would tell you. Fugging clocksuckin' motherfriggin' life.

And life hurts like a bitch.

Head pounding; eyes smarting from something; his lungs knocking back big bushels of air as if someone had been trying to smother him.

Maybe the bastards had.

Maybe they left him for dead.

Maybe they were still gonna kill him.

He thought just about fifty things in the space of a minute or two, and then sat up.

Bald Hill was just up along the path; he could see the lights of the towers of school beyond the scraggly trees. For a brief disoriented moment, he was pretty sure that maybe he'd imagined all the crap with the other students in the dark. But his sides hurt enough, and as the seconds passed, he knew that what had just happened was real.

A clean, frosty breeze made him shiver, and the fallen leaves scuttled around the graves. He knew the area well, as he'd often wandered there to study on a bright and clear afternoon; or had gone out with Fricker and Tippy, who tended to jones for cigarettes just after supper. Sometimes the seniors dragged freshmen out in the dark of the moon and scared the living shit out of them with tales of Harrow terror and then kicked their butts all the way back to their rooms.

He looked up at the night sky. It was clear and brilliant with stars against an indigo darkness.

The moonlight cast a translucent sheen across the graves.

The old mausoleum of the Gravesends, the family that built the original Harrow House, rose before him, its cast-iron gate open. Expecting his tormenters to be standing there around him, he glanced around quickly, his back and head aching as if he'd been drunk.

He stood, after a few moments of trying, on wobbly feet. The lamps on either side of the mausoleum flickered; he glanced about, but no shadows lurked.

Yet they might be watching him.

Waiting to see his next move.

He walked unsteadily toward the mausoleum. It was of the same white stone as the two residential houses. He had been out here dozens of times, generally trying to break in to the crypt. But this time the chain was down; the lock was open.

They've done this, he thought. *They've laid a trap. Or they want me to go down into the crypt.*

Or they're watching. If I go down there, they'll lock me in for the night. If I don't go down, I'll have failed the test.

Yep, my choices suck.

"Face everything," he whispered to himself. It was one of their sayings. Christ, who are they? Who the hell are they? Why didn't they want him to see them? What the hell was going on? Part of him wanted to cry like a little kid; part of him wanted to kick the Honor Council, Kelleher, and these Invisibles in the balls.

Then he repeated this more clearly, loud, into the night: "Face everything. All right. I'm going. You kicked me in the butt, but I'm going to go. If that's the test."

He spun around, hoping to catch a glimpse of one of them.

He stood for a moment, facing the scraggly woods and the graves, and said as loud as he could, "I don't want to be kicked out. I have to stay here. I'll do this. Okay? I'll do it."

Then, Jim Hook went to the entrance of the mausoleum. It was pitch black inside. Waiting for him on the steps: a large flashlight.

2

The steps down were worn and slippery; damp scum of some kind covered them. Jim took them slowly, one at a time, until he reached the fifth step down, and then he was in the crypt.

He shined the flashlight around—various names were on the graves, and two table graves rose at the center of the marble floor.

Jim made sure that no one was lurking in any corner of the crypt. Then he went to the great slabs that lay on top of the two graves in the middle of the small, square room. He shined the light upon one.

It read:

Mischief

Genevieve Campion Gravesend. Born to grace and to beauty, daughter of Claude and Rachel Campion, wife of Justin Gravesend III, mother to Alan Gravesend. Died at her beloved Balmoral Cottage, Fenwick, Connecticut, during the year of our Lord 1891.

A bas-relief rose at the foot of the crypt, of a curious but beautiful angel, with wings that seemed to come from its scalp and sweep along its shoulders.

The angel's face was distinct—not a generic carving of the divine, but a specific face, with a sharp but not unpleasant nose, eyes like almonds, and a weak chin that did nothing to detract from the beauty of the face as a whole. Even more curious, some kind of ring was on the wedding finger of the statue.

Jim guessed that the sculptor had created a marble angel from a portrait of Genevieve Gravesend.

Jim turned the light on the other sarcophagus. It was perfectly smooth alabaster. He touched the stone, and felt its ice. There was no name, no image, nothing upon it. He set the flashlight on Genevieve's crypt, its light aimed for the edge of the other's lid. Lid? That's what it seemed to him.

It was the doorway to Death, and he had to open it.

Okay. I can do that.

He pressed his fingers beneath the slab, but it didn't budge. His wrist ached from the effort.

He lifted the flashlight again, and directed the beam to the walls. There were a few graves on the wall, but someone had written across the wall in what might've been blood:

WAIT FOR WHAT WILL COME.

He shined the light along the other walls, but there were no other messages left for him.

"Wait for what will come," he said aloud. *Journey with Us into Enlightenment, and Wait for What Will Come. The school motto. Not too friggin' original.*

He went over to the wall and touched the wet paint of the writing. Instinctively, he brought his fingers to his nose to sniff the paint. Briefly, he let the tip of his tongue taste his fingertip.

The bitter taste of copper.

"Holy shit," he gasped. It may have been his imagination, but it reminded him of the taste of blood.

He almost dropped the flashlight; its beam hit an object on the floor.

It looked like a human finger.

He *had* to pick it up.

Chapter Sixteen
A Small Gift

Jim was sure it was a trick, just like the blood on the wall. After all, it might be someone's blood. Someone very much alive and cutting themselves just so they could put some blood up on the wall.

"All right, a lot of blood," he admitted aloud.

He crouched down, and grabbed the finger. A school signet ring was attached to it. It felt like a mushy worm.

He put the light up against it. It had to be a fake.

It had to.

But no, in fact, it had that squishiness of human flesh and bone, and perhaps worst of all:

It seemed fresh.

Douglas Clegg

The words they'd said came back to him:
We are one hand. A hand needs all its fingers.
If you find something that seems unusual, keep it to yourself. It's from us. A small gift.

When he got back to his room in the Trenches that night, he quickly stuck the finger behind his underwear in the bottom drawer of the slim dresser that stood at the foot of his bed.

He slipped beneath the sheets, too stunned to even take his jacket off, and fell asleep.

That's when the scratching began, and he heard the wood of the attic door splintering.

Chapter Seventeen
Small Miracles

1

Jim was on his way to the showers, his towel around his waist, Ivory soap bar in one hand, Prell shampoo tucked underneath his armpit, when he noticed the small square of paper.

Someone had slipped a pink piece of paper under Jim's door—it was a message from the veterinary clinic in town telling him his puppy was ready to be picked up.

"It ain't mine," he said, balling the slip of paper up and dropping it in the trash after he'd showered up and shaved what little facial stubble had grown in the past twenty-four hours.

Then, as he dressed, he even felt guilty about

the puppy, and, remembering his promise to Lark, tried to call the vet's office, only he got put on hold too long and it was almost 7:30 A.M., so he had less than twenty minutes to get to the dining hall and grab something.

He was starving.

2

Jim ate too much at breakfast—it was as if his appetite were bigger than ever, and he even went back for seconds on eggs and toast, and when he felt completely filled to bursting, he went and spewed it all up in the toilet. Looking at himself in the bathroom mirror, his lips cracked with dryness, his hair all screwed up and all over the place and sticking out from the sides of his scalp like a deranged mad scientist, he tried not to remember that his life was just about over at Harrow.

He tried not to see Stephen in his face.

Stephen, taller, handsomer, smarter, less likely to get thrown out on an honor violation.

Jim splashed cold water on his face and swore that he was going to make it all work somehow. "Do not let the bastards get you down," he said aloud to his reflection of blood-shot eyes and bloodshot soul.

3

The headmaster called Jim into his office just before the bell rang for first period.

The headmaster, Mr. Trimalchio, was tall and thick and looked like he had once played rugby and squash and all the rich boy sports before turning to the life of the mind. He was in his late forties, in the kind of physical condition some of the boys envied. His mustache was pepper gray, his eyes wise orbs, and his manner very nearly kind.

The assumption was that Trimalchio had once been quite handsome and lively, for there were photos from past yearbooks that could be hunted down in the library's stack room—and in all of them, Jay Trimalchio was the golden boy of the football team and a prize wrestler and head of the yearbook staff as well as Honor Student four years running. He had gone to Dartmouth, but had graduated from a lesser known college on Long Island, New York; his master's came via Rutgers; and then, within a few years, he was back at Harrow.

Then, the boys assumed, something had happened.

For how, after all, would a handsome, rich graduate of Harrow end up back in the 'Row as if it were as impossible to escape this place as Alcatraz and Sing Sing combined? There was nothing about Trimalchio that seemed dumb, and yet he had never really left the building.

Trimalchio had remained at the school since his late twenties, and now, in his forties, he seemed as entrenched as St. George–and–Dragon in the front drive. Thus, most of the boys had dubbed him a loser, and Bilge had gone so far as to declare during study hall—when the proctor was gone for a minute—that Trimalchio was a queer. Or a pervert. Or he was one of those old men who chase girls all their lives. Or he got off on watching boys in the locker room, or someone had cut his balls off.

Something—anything—to explain why he'd stayed at Harrow throughout his life.

But Jim forgot about anything regarding the headmaster other than the fact that his future was now in this man's hands.

4

Trimalchio thrummed the yellow pad on his desk, and watched Jim with some kind of care. Jim felt like he was in the presence of a priest. He had just recently gotten a haircut that made him look absolutely well tended. "You're in luck, Mr. Hook," the headmaster said.

"Sir?" Jim shifted uncomfortably in his chair. His tie felt like a noose around his neck; his shirt felt overstarched, and itched when he moved. He was far too conscious of the tight-

ness of his underwear and the jittery six-cups-
of-coffee feeling in his head.

"We can't call the Honor Council. Sam
DeGroot, Sergeant-at-Arms, came down with
something yesterday. Food poisoning. Assuming he'll be well enough, we'll convene at two-
fifteen on Friday in the Council Room in West.
I advise you not to speak of this to anyone, nor
are you to seek advice from your peers or instructors. Your lips should be sealed on this
matter, as will all of ours. Do not compound the
charge brought against you with another."

"Yes, sir." Jim nodded. "And sir?"

"Mr. Hook?"

"I don't want to leave Harrow."

"No one does, Mr. Hook. I won't pass judg-
ment on what I've been told. It is up to the
Council of your peers. But I will say, given your
brother's record here, I would be ashamed were
I you. I'm even sorry to have to say this to you.
I have some confidence that the charge against
you is inaccurate."

"Sir, I assure you that—"

"Enough, Mr. Hook." Trimalchio nodded.
"You'll need to keep to your room after classes.
You are to discuss this case with no one, not
even Matthew Meloni. Clear?"

"Yes, sir." Jim managed to rise from the chair
without toppling it over in shame and embar-
rassment. But still, he felt relief. He looked at

the brass plaque above Trimalchio's ornate desk.

On it, a list of the top students from each class for the past twenty years.

He imagined he could make out his brother's name near the bottom.

5

He looked at the other students differently.

Bilge, with his overly obnoxious farts and the way he laughed over all the wrong things and then acted as if he were everyone's victim, and hated anything that involved physical activity. Fricker—sure, Trey Fricker was pretty close to being his best friend at school, but maybe that's why he got picked at all.

Yeah, that was it.

Fricker was inducting him into this warped group of liars, cheaters, and stealers. Fricker always kept things to himself. Of course it was Fricker.

Naw, not Fricker. Yeah, maybe Fricker. Who knows?

Michael-the-Good. Now, there was a guy with something to hide. Nobody was that saintly, not at fifteen. Nobody *never* got in trouble that much. Who else but a saint to have the best cover for midnight activities like this shadow group?

Or Shrike—Shrike was an asshole from the

word go. But he was too stupid for this kind of thing. He got disqualified right there. Shrike wasn't smart enough to know how to create some kind of secret society.

Tippy Tipton? Wimpy, but smart. Maybe that's what it took.

Griff. Maybe? No. Well, perhaps.

What if it were Kip French?

Bryn.

McNally.

Hardass and Bleeder both.

Even Mojo. Any one of them could be part of the group of thugs who had ambushed him. Their faces spun in his mind as he tried to figure out which ones might be part of this . . . this . . . cabal.

Who? Which ones? He tried to listen for their voices; tried to identify them in some way. Whom had he sensed, there in the dark? Who was most likely to be part of this group?

Even the seventh grader, Miles, little Mole that he was—the one he'd only just met at gym glass the morning of his disgrace. Even that kid seemed different now. Jim passed him as the mad hall rush began after Bio, and the corridor in East was a sea of middle-schoolers as Jim made his way around the building to get out to the courtyard for free period.

Miles looked at him in a funny way, the kid's eyes widening slightly. Miles's eyes flashed something—understanding? Collusion? What?

For a second, Jim had the distinct feeling that Miles didn't expect to see him at all this particular day.

He's heard, Jim thought as he watched Miles glance back at him one more time before being swallowed up in the tide headed for the classrooms.

Christ, it could be anyone. My best friend. Some kid.

He almost stopped in his tracks when he felt a shiver run up his spine. Someone was staring at him. He was almost to the double doors of East, almost out to the Courtyard, and he felt someone watching him.

Turn around. Face him. Whoever it is. It doesn't matter. Don't be scared.

Face everything.

He turned quickly, but the hall was empty of all but a few stragglers.

Jim Hook felt utterly alone.

6

"You are screwed like the Queen of England is screwed, boy: *Royally.*" Trey Fricker shook his head slowly, the trickle of a laugh in his words. "Damn."

He was out back behind the arches, leaning against one of the numerous rubbles of stone, weeds growing all around him as if he'd been planted there, cigarette between his lips.

"Thanks."

Fricker laughed so hard he almost spat out the cigarette. "No, don't take it the wrong way. This kind of crap happens here. What are you gonna do?"

"I guess get kicked out. Christ." Jim swiped his hand over his scalp, imagining that his hair came out in his fingers. "All last night, I barely slept. This is bad. It's just bad. Why did I even look at your paper?"

Fricker drew the cigarette from his mouth, tapping it against a rock. "You actually looked at my paper?"

"You were there. You know I did. You let me see it," Jim said.

Fricker waved his cig around like it was a pointer. "You think I would do that? No. Nope. I did not. I didn't even know you were looking. You looked at my paper? Jimmy Jimmy Jimmy." Fricker took another whooping inhale of smoke and coughed it out. "Well, rules is rules, as they say."

"Who makes those rules?"

Fricker looked at him as if he were crazy. "It's the rule. You cheated. They caught you. The Honor Code is important here. I know it seems old-fashioned, but hey, even I sort of believe it."

"You didn't catch me. Christ, who did? And anyway, you've broken the rules, too."

"How?"

Douglas Clegg

"You're talking about it with me. That's violating the code, too."

"Uh, Hook, that may be true, but you don't get kicked out for that."

"I'm screwed," Jim sighed. He put his hand out. "Gimme a cig, will ya?"

"One last smoke for the condemned man." Fricker grinned. He brought the pack of Winstons from his pocket and tossed it to him. "You can have the rest. Jesus, that Carrington."

"Hugh?" Jim began puffing on the cigarette like it was pure oxygen and he'd been smothering. Then the coughing fit came. "Christ, why does anyone smoke?"

"Keep smoking and you'll find out. And yeah, Hugh Pukin' Carrington was the squealer. I heard his voice loud and clear. He'll be the one giving testimony, no doubt. You know what? You should get to him."

"What do you mean, get to him?"

"Get to him. You know. Get to him," Fricker grinned, stubbing out the last of his cigarette. He glanced at his wristwatch. "I got Latin in five. What's up for you?"

"Study hall."

"Think about it," Fricker said, rising, brushing his slacks off. "If I was in your shoes, I'd try to get Carrington. And damn, Hook, don't keep talking about this. You'll fuck it up." Jim could not stop staring at the fourth finger of Fricker's right hand, with Fricker's class ring wrapped

178

around it. Fricker noticed, and lifted his hand up. "You like? My dad ordered it for me. It's squirrelly, but hell, it gives me a little pride in the 'Row to have it."

7

Jim had not managed to put the finger out of his mind. He rolled it around in his head, and could practically see the finger rolling. Whose finger was it? Was it some kind of trick? Was it a fake finger that just felt real?

Once the school day was over, he went back to his room and drew it out. It had bled a little, which surprised him, on his Fruit of the Looms. Just a few drops of bright red blood.

It was a finger, with the nail torn off.

A real finger. He didn't want to examine it too much, but he had to see if there really was a bone in there. That would prove it once and for all. Using a thumbtack from the cork board above Meloni's bed, Jim pulled back some of the skin.

Sure enough: a small white lump of bone.

Finger bone.

He felt the threat of vomit at the back of his throat. After having lost breakfast, but managing to keep his lunch down, he didn't want to let anything else come up. He took a few deep breaths.

Okay. So it's a finger. Maybe it's from some

179

dead guy. Some guy from maybe the mortuary in town. Maybe that was all. Or maybe it was from something else. I mean, there wasn't that much blood. It might be an old, old finger. It was in a crypt. It was from some dead guy. They cut it off as a joke or a trick. That was the kind of thing these guys probably did to scare people off. It was morbid and gross, but he wouldn't put it past half the assholes in school to do that kind of thing.

He went and washed his hands; then he sat down on his bed, and picked the finger up again.

The ring around it was a school signet. He took the ring off, and examined it.

Inside the ring, the inscription: *Stephen Hook, Class of '95.*

Yet it was not his brother's finger.

Plus, his brother had not had that ring. Not precisely. It had been lost; Jim knew it had been lost, because Stephen, then a Junior, whined about losing it. His mother was furious with him, because the ring had cost good money; but his father did not mind, and told his mother that there were other rings the boy would have in the world.

His father always had that tender way of speaking to his mother.

It was something Jim missed about him.

He could practically see his father's face: It was nearly unlined at forty, his hairline had receded a bit, and there was a frosting of gray along his short-cut sandy brown hair, turning the ends to silver. His eyes were youthful and twinkly, and even when angered, his father had managed to keep a look about him of calm and patience. Even when the seas got rough (that's what his father, raised on sailing, had said), he kept his hands on the rudder.

Jim couldn't conjure his brother's face; and his eyes blurred. All that had happened within the past two days clutched at his throat. He felt stirring, like someone plucking at strings beneath his skin.

He sat on his small bed, alone in his dormitory room, and stared at the green walls. His eyes felt as if they were burning; he was sure that he was going to have a heart attack. As crazy as it sounded, he felt his heart beating in his chest, and it seemed to thump louder and more violently than usual. His neck felt stiff, and his back ached.

Whatever mess he'd gotten himself into, it wasn't going to go away.

8

"I've been waiting for your call."

"Sorry," Jim said, sounding less smooth than he wanted to. He glanced at his wristwatch. It was just after five P.M. The other guys were horsing around in the hall, so it was hard to hear Lark's voice. "Hey," he said, cupping his hand over the receiver. "Shut the hell up, will ya?"

Then, back to the hall phone. "I meant to call earlier, only I got wound up in some stuff."

"Hey, how's the dog?"

"Dog?"

"The Great Pup Caper," Lark said, brightly. Then, "We told the vet we'd check in before the weekend." Her voice sank a bit. "You didn't call the office?"

"Oh, yeah. I tried calling this morning but got put on hold. And I've been busy. I'll go look in on the muttly tomorrow."

"He's not a muttly."

"He's a muttly mange of a pup. But I'll check in on the son of a bitch tomorrow," Jim promised.

"Aw, that poor puppy. And you calling him bad things. Okay if I come up Friday night? Jenny wants to see Rich, and we can borrow her car and go to the movies or something if we want after they hook up."

"Sure. Yeah. Sure."

"Something up? You sound funny."

He hesitated. *Better not tell her.* "Naw. Just have a lot of tests this week. You know the drill."

"Tell me about it. I'm having a crappy week myself. I had chemistry this morning. I had no idea the elements were so, well, elemental. I probably flunked it."

"No, you probably aced it."

"I bet I flunked. How'd Western Civ go?"

A momentary silence on the line. Then he said, "Okay. I probably flunked that one, too."

"You underestimate yourself all the time. You probably passed with flying colors."

"Yeah. Maybe. Doubt it."

The conversation felt tense. He didn't like lying to her. But he just didn't want to get into what had happened with the midterm. "I can't wait to see you Friday. I miss you already."

"Aw. Thank you. No one else seems to miss me. Oh, darn it—I better go, Jim. I'm getting signals from Marti that she wants the phone."

"Okay. See you Friday."

"All right. All right," she said, not to him, but to her roommate, and then the dial tone came up. He looked at the phone, and then hung it back up on the wall.

He felt like the biggest jerk in the world for not at least telling the truth.

Jim Hook wished he could erase the world back to Sunday night when he was kissing her and rescuing puppies and running through the rain feeling as if, for once in his life, things were headed in the right direction.

Chapter Eighteen
Lark at St. Cat's

1

Lark Trotter passed the cell phone to her roommate, and was out the door of the dorm room, letting it slam less than gently behind her. There was this thing with Lark: She wanted to win too badly, in any situation. It wasn't a pretty quality, she knew.

And she didn't win most of the time. That was her other problem.

Her roommate, Marti Hofstedter, was a real bitch, and had practically turned her in the night before for breaking curfew. Lark had to bribe her with doing her English term paper on "Animal Imagery in Shakespeare," which was due in two weeks and for which Lark would now have to spend half her free time rereading "A Midsummer Night's Dream" just to figure out what the hell she was going to write about. And she had wanted to try out for the school play, too, but between seeing Jim on the weekends and now her virtual slavery to Marti over a six-page paper (which seemed unimaginable since most of the papers they had to write were two to three typed pages), it was not shaping up like a good week.

Lark was not going to win this week.

She was in a terrible mood, and the worst part of it was she had wanted to appear so sweet to Jim on the phone, but felt that she was channeling Marti or one of Marti's nasty friends.

Then, of course, she'd barely gotten any sleep the night before, which didn't help—the alarm had gone off at seven, and she'd had to rush to the showers just to get a place in line, and even so, she was late for first period.

And then, there was that note, which pissed her off but good.

She didn't even want to think about it. It was just some nasty human being who had nothing better to do than play some nasty head game with her, and if she had to guess which rat it was, it might've been any number of the rats at Harrow Academy.

And this hall. This dorm. This school. Everything.

The hall was a mess—none of the girls ever kept it the least bit clean until the weekend, and Hally Cromwell was on resident duty, which meant it would remain a mess through the next few days until the end of October, when someone else got assigned.

"Jen!" Lark called, striding down the hall, feeling a bad nervous energy just from Jim's voice. Something was definitely up—it practically spat over the phone line with electric force—but she hadn't been about to wheedle it out of him. They had dated a few weeks, and she was falling too fast; even she knew it. He was a year younger than she, he wouldn't even have his driver's license until spring or summer, and what would happen? There was something unnerving at times about him, too, but she just could not help herself. She wanted to spend as much spare time over at Harrow with him as she could. She wished she could borrow Jenny's car and just take off to see him that night, but it wasn't going to work.

And anyway, she had too much to get done. She had her own essay to write on imagery in "Macbeth," and then she was supposed to start memorizing that prologue from *The Canterbury Tales*, which sounded silly in Middle English, but it was one of those St. Catherine's requirements. And then that damn paper for blackmailer Marti. "All St. Catherine's graduates will have committed Chaucer's Prologue to memory by the time they leave these halls," so commanded Suky Shultz, the young, far too chipper Junior Honors English teacher. Suky had been a graduate of St. Cat's, as had her mother and aunt. Then, she had returned after studying at Middlebury and the Sorbonne and even had a Fulbright Scholarship in London after all that—and still, she'd returned to St. Cat's, as did more than a few college graduates for a year or two of teaching.

"Whan that Aprille with it shoures sootah," Lark said as she walked down the hall, trying to remember more than one line from the *Canterbury Tales* prologue. Then, *"Jen!"*

Jenny's door was open, but she had her headphones on. When she saw Lark, she held up her index finger.

"I distinctly smell pot in this room," Lark said, coughing. "Open the windows, come on, you're gonna get tossed out." She stepped back out of the room and leaned against the wall. Pembroke Wallis and Nancy Shipman waltzed in like the twinsies they were, with their identical skirts and identical sparkling blond hair.

Lark rapped on the wall. "Come on, Jen, let's go."

Jenny was hooked on Beck, who brought her out of her not-infrequent depressions. Usually she played an album of his over and over again. Sometimes she smoked pot with a half dozen fans turned up and a towel under the door crack. That was one aspect of Jenny that Lark had never liked. "You're going to be a head, a stoner, a wastrel," she'd tell her.

"It makes me think more clearly," Jenny would tell her and then, stoned, drift off to some other thought or plane of existence.

Lark waited in the hall—everyone who went by on the way to dinner annoyed her, and she realized one of the reasons was that it was going to be time for what Jen called the Dreaded Visitor, and that didn't help matters, because it meant she'd be popping Midol and being grumbly until Thursday at least—if she were lucky.

Within a few minutes, Jenny came out, smoothing her blouse and skirt, brushing the crumbs of some previously devoured graham crackers onto the floor.

"Ready for supper?"

"Always," Jenny said.

"You need a sweater. You're gonna freeze."

Jenny ignored her. She playfully pushed Lark onward, out of the dorm, into the quad. The lights had come up too bright—squintingly bright—since the days had begun darkening early. It was like stadium lighting—it made the quad look two-dimensional in the broad, flat light.

When they were halfway down the walk toward the cafeteria, Lark stopped and grabbed her hand. "I have to tell you something."

"Shoot," Jenny said.

"I got this today." Lark reached into her breast pocket and withdrew a small, torn piece of paper. "I talked with him tonight but I didn't . . . I didn't really mention it."

She passed it over to Jenny, and when Jenny looked at it, her brows knit on her forehead. "This is just sick. Oh, Lark. Jeez, who coulda wrote this?"

"I don't know."

"Well, it's obviously not true."

"You think?" Lark managed a smile.

"Oh my god, yeah. Good gravy," Jenny said. She always said corny things like that. *Good gravy. Cheese and crackers. Dagnab it. Jinx on a Coke.* It made her sweeter in Lark's eyes, because once, when Jenny got really mad after Alice Garver made a crack about her weight, Jenny had just exploded with the foulest language that had ever been heard in the halls of St. Cat's—which was saying a lot. "Jimmy isn't this kind of guy. I know it. I know people, Lark. Didn't he just rescue a puppy? Boys who rescue puppies don't have anything to do with this kind of crapola."

"Yeah."

"And he's never done anything remotely like this, right?"

Lark nodded.

"So." Jenny glanced back at the note in the light; she squinted. "Who wrote this piece of trash?"

"I have no idea. It was in this little envelope in my mailbox when I got out of French today. Someone mailed it yesterday. From Watch Point." She began to feel flustered all over again, as she had the minute she'd opened the envelope and read the note the first time. And then again. And again. Until her imagination had just gone too wild. "It's like a stalker note. Who would write it? Why me? Why use his name?"

"You didn't ask him?"

"What would he say? He'd be embarrassed and angry that someone had even done this. And then, he'd know. You know. That I'd read it. That for a second, I might've even thought it."

"Guess so." Jenny wadded the note up. "It was probably Shreve Boucher. He's the type. Or Carrington. What a dick that guy is. He's after you, too. I can tell. He has been since ninth grade. You don't think it's Charlie, do you?"

"Maybe. I don't know. No. No, Charlie wouldn't do that. I doubt even Shreve would." Lark shivered. "What kind of boy writes that kind of thing and sends it—let alone thinks it?"

"Ooh, maybe it's just some pervert who saw you with him," Jenny said, and then shook her head. "Nope. It's probably just one of those jerks. Remember what Coop did last year to Trish Pepper? Harrow always has a few psychos in its midst. Well, forget it. I seriously doubt

191

that our Jimmy boy is the kind of guy to do that stuff or make up crap. But those other preppie-heads-up-their-asses Harrow hard-ons, yeah, I could believe it of almost any of them," Jenny said, and then she nudged Lark. "Now, let's go. I hear they're serving train wreck for dinner, with a little squirrel on the side."

2

The note:

> Dear Lark bitch,
> Your little boyfriend Jimbo told all of us how your pussy smells like tuna salad with lots of mayo and how he already had you fifty ways to Sunday and how he's going to share you with all of us come this weekend, you fucking whore.
> I can't wait to taste your juicy juicy red red rosy portal of pleasure. Jimbo said it was scrumpdiddlyumptious.
>
> > Love always,
> > your secret admirer in hell

Chapter Nineteen
Something's Coming Through

1

Hugh Carrington was what the teachers thought of as a pure Harrow student.

He had come to Harrow in the seventh grade from St. Anselm's, the Episcopal Elementary School in Crossfield, Connecticut, with high marks and an early aptitude for sports and mathematics. His hair was honey-blond, he was strong and handsome, he rowed crew in the summers with the Academy Achievers, a small group of upperclassmen who intended to get in to Ivy League schools and excel in every way. It was getting to be time for the dinner bell, but he had just gotten out of football practice, and decided to skip dinner and go for a jog along Hadrian's Wall at the back of campus.

The brisk air felt good—it was nearly October, and the Hudson spewed up a magnificent stench as he tried to keep his pace regular to avoid cramps and the exhaustion that generally accompanied an after-practice sprint.

Twilight had darkened with the oncoming night, and the purplish hues of the river and the hills rising from its opposite bank were calming for him as he ran. Leaves crunched beneath his feet, and the last bird calls would continue; geese flew in formation overhead; the world was a good place for boys like Hugh.

He took the more difficult path when he reached the woods, the one that went in among the trees, and that was Hugh Carrington's first mistake.

His second mistake was stopping among the trees, feeling as if someone were watching him.

His third mistake was going deeper into the woods to find out who exactly was there.

2

Hugh's mind worked like this: He came, he saw, he conquered, just like the Latin lesson about Caesar, and he wasn't about to let some jerk-off like Shrike or Coop play those freak tricks on him like they had during baseball practice the previous spring. It was one thing to get some goony cheerleader from Watch Point High to come over hanging her tits out and carrying a big old crate of what were supposed to be hash brownies but turned out to be Ex-Lax brownies just so he'd be crapping his pants when he was pitching from the mound, but it was another to be following him and trying to make him all paranoid.

Hugh Carrington was not going to put up with that kind of shit.

"Come on, Shrike, get your butt out here, you pussy," he said, and jumped over some brambles, off the path, and into the woods. He deftly avoided the potholes of nature—the rocks and fern outgrowths that hadn't quite died with autumn, the slick piles of leaves that covered the earth. He had to duck under some branches, but he caught sight of the kid who was standing there—

"Who are you, you stupid son of a bitch," he spat as he came to a small clearing with a thicket at its center. "Come out now so I can break your face."

A boy of about eleven or twelve emerged from the thicket, only as he got closer to him, Hugh Carrington began shivering—

His eyes—

Dark, as if there were no eyes at all, but shaded, empty sockets—

And then when the boy came closer, he showed Hugh Carrington something terrible.

195

Hugh felt the piss run down his jockstrap, soaking his running shorts, but this was replaced by the absolute chill—

The ice of knowing something he wasn't supposed to know.

Foam poured from between his lips, and he felt something scrambling in his head—

Knowing—

Not knowing what others knew, but knowing something—

Witnessing something—

That human eyes were never meant to witness—

His blood began boiling within his skin—

He smelled something that might've been burning meat—

The boy revealed all to Hugh Carrington.

Chapter Twenty
Drunk!

1

"Call for you," Meloni said, shaking him on his shoulder. "Hook. Come on. Get up."

Jim awoke slowly—it seemed minutes had passed before he stopped feeling groggy. He eyed his roommate suspiciously. "What's up?"

"Call for you. In the hall."

"Who? Lark?"

"Didn't ask. Sounds like your mom," Meloni said, and tossed his books over on his bed. "What—you napped through supper?"

"Yeah." Jim felt sticky and sweaty, and wanted to wash himself off. He sat up.

"You better get out there before she hangs up."

"Who?" he said, sleepily.

"Your mom. How many times do I have to say it?"

2

"Mom?"

Pause.

"Mom?"

"I'm here," she finally said. He could imagine her, sitting on the flower-print sofa with a cup of coffee beside her, and the evening news on the television but without the sound. "Did you get the letter I sent?"

"Letter? No. Not yet. I didn't check yet, though. Is something wrong?"

"No," she said, her voice slightly hoarse. "All right, I got a call last night."

"Call?"

"A phone call. Someone called and told me something." She sighed into the phone. "I'm sure it's only some prank. Probably one of the boys. I'm sure they just got the number from the student handbook."

"Someone called you? Last night?"

"I . . . they said something strange. It was the strangest thing. This person—well, it had to be one of your friends or some prankster up there—this person said that you . . . Well, this is ridiculous. It doesn't matter what they said. It just got me to thinking about the letter I sent the day before yesterday."

"What did they tell you on the phone?"

His mother ignored him. She waited a moment, and then continued. "It's something I found the other day. I was cleaning up a little, going through the trunks in storage, trying to find some of your father's things, just thinking I'd come across—you know which ones I mean—those really elegant cuff links he had from Spain. And when I was going through things, I found something that I thought you should have."

"What was it?"

"Oh, I should let you be surprised. You'll be surprised," she said, laughing nervously. "I don't want to spoil it. How's school going?"

"Fine. Mom, what are you sending?"

"If I tell you, it won't be a surprise. Let's just say it's something that you'll cherish when you see it."

He blurted it out. "Is it his ring?"

He heard his mother catch her breath.

"Is it Stephen's class ring? With his name engraved on the inside? Is that what you sent?" Jim was only dimly aware of how his voice rose slightly, almost aggressively.

His mother went silent. He could hear a siren in the background. She was sitting by the window, with the blinds drawn but the windows open wide. It was how she kept things in the apartment: blinds always drawn.

Then she said, "Of course it's not his ring. Why in god's name would you guess that? My god."

The silence on the phone was replaced by the barking of some dog in the neighborhood where his mother lived; the echoes of traffic and boom boxes.

"Are you all right, Mom?"

"I'll . . . I'll be fine in a minute. What you said. It just brought back that night for me."

"I'm sorry. I'm not sure why I guessed the ring. I know he lost it."

"He found it again," she said, swiftly. "That night. He found it and he wore it. It's been enough years, you'd think this wouldn't bother me. Something like that ring. The way his fingers . . . I'm sorry, Jimmy. I don't mean to be this upset."

"Mom? His fingers?"

"Jim, I have to go. I can't run up the phone bill this month. Look, I'll put some money in the mail for you. It's not much, but it'll make it so you and your girl can go out to the movies or something."

"I wish you wouldn't send it, Mom. I'm doing fine. And I've got work in the Development office and the kitchen on weekends, so it's not like I'm completely broke."

"You should have a little fun," she said.

"I do. Don't send me the money. Okay?"

She hesitated. "If you say so. All right. I'll hold it."

He wanted to jump in with, *And Mom, you don't go without a meal just so I can have an extra twenty dollars, do you?* But he didn't want to believe it, he didn't want to know if it was true. The thought of his mother skipping lunch or dinner just so he could have pocket change upset him. He knew it couldn't be true. And how would the others know that anyway? How could they know?

"You sure everything is fine there?"

"Yeah, Mom. Yes. It is. Really."

"Good. Prank phone calls," his mother tsked. "I guess boys do those kinds of things. Well, keep an eye out for that envelope. I miss you."

"Yeah, me too, Mom."

"You sure you're not in any trouble?"

"Positive. Good night, Mom."

"Night, Jim. And Jim . . ."

"Still here."

"He'd be proud of you. You know that. You don't need me telling you that."

He stared at the telephone in the hall for a moment before hanging it up. Tears overcame him. He felt like a three-year-old lost at a shopping mall. He couldn't let the other guys see it— if anyone came down the hall, he'd look like a pathetic loser who couldn't handle himself. That's pretty much what the other kids thought of criers. He wasn't going to be thought of that way. He wasn't going to leave himself that open to the bastards.

He felt as if he had never learned anything in all his life.

He might as well be dead.

It was over for him.

Between the bullies who had beat the crap out of him, and the Honor Council, he felt as if he might as well go to the roof and just jump.

3

The handbook:

The duties of the Honor Council are three-fold. It must educate the academic and so-cial community about the Honor Code and its meaning such that no student will mis-understand its importance and reach. In-tegrity is at its core, and a solid notion of what is right and what is wrong are its crown and scepter. Also, it is the realm of the Honor Council to enforce the Code by speedily calling hearings should there be an accusation of an Honor Violation, and by investigating without prejudice any such case should one arise.

Lastly, it must instill in each member of the Harrow community a sense of the eternal truth of Honor. It is not to be breached or compromised in any way, shape, or form.

The Honor Council deals with all such investigations in absolute confidence, with complete anonymity for both the accused and the accuser(s). When an Honor Trial must be conducted in order to bring the light of justice to bear upon such an accusation, the accused shall be duly informed of all alleged mischief on his part by a designated teacher or the Headmaster or the Disciplinary Counseler. Such authority shall then call a meeting with the accused to outline the ramifications of the accusation.

At this time, it will be suggested to the accused to contact his parent or guardian for further guidance, should the violation move to Trial.

4

He couldn't eat that night. Now, thoughts of his mother were making his head throb and his ears ring, and his stomach felt like it was full of butterflies getting drowned in gastric acid. *Poor Mom. Christ, poor Mom. Up in Yonkers putting on a show so I'll feel comfortable here. And me just taking, taking, taking. Christ, I shouldn't even be here. Poor boys don't go to rich boys' schools.*

It's absurd.

Ridiculous.

Crazy.

He drank some of the vodka that Mojo kept hidden in his green canvas duffel bag full of dirty laundry. Mojo had a Dixie cup full, but Jim ended up just swigging from the bottle.

"You're a terrible drunk," Mojo said with far too much sincerity. He motioned for the bottle. "Come on, hand it over. You're bogarting it too much. You're gonna get sick."

"I don't care. I don't give a rat's ass."

"Now you're talkin'." Mojo lip-farted. "Put the bottle down. Jim. Put. The. Bottle. Down."

"I've been here, what? A total of a semester and maybe a half? Maybe? A half? And what—I have my dad and bro to thank for being such perfect—you know they weren't such perfect—they been bad—very, very bad," Jim said, thinking that he was headed somewhere with this profound thought, but the room spun a little and it seemed to spin his thoughts out into space.

"Drink much?" Mojo laughed, finally wrestling the Stolichnaya from him. "Keerist, Hook, you done drank half the bottle."

"I did?" Jim grinned, feeling vaguely proud. "I hope the cops don't find out."

"The cops," Mojo laughed. "Yeah, they're gonna throw your butt in jail."

"Drunk tank." Jim laughed a little too loud. A few minutes later, he was throwing up in the sink, and Mojo held a wet handtowel to the back of his neck.

"Take it easy," Mojo said.

Jim was afraid he had just been telling Mojo about the finger and the shadow students who roughed him up and read him their manifesto, but he was too drunk to be sure if he had actually said something or imagined it.

He began babbling, tears and sweat and cuss words pushing their way out from his body in one way or another. "I can't take this bullshit anymore, this utter and complete bullshit, I am never gonna be Stephen and I'm never gonna bring them back and my mom can cry and sacrifice and be Mrs. Martyr all she wants, but I don't need this bullshit, this absolute bullshit, all this bullybullyshitshit."

Then the world spun like a carousel ride. He saw the room and its contents blur. Mojo seemed to grow six eyes, and some compact disc was playing from some room—it sounded like jazz but not the kind he liked, the kind that was like a trumpet solo with a cello in the background and a drum beat—and then every corner of the room began to creep with inky blackness until all the dots met and he passed out.

When he regained consciousness, it was pitch
black. He could hear Mojo's snores from the
nearby bed. Jim was in his bed, lying there in
his briefs, his mouth tasting like a cat's hind-
quarters, and his head pounding with a jack-
hammer. He checked the green light of the
digital alarm clock—it was 2 A.M.

It's always 2 A.M. for me.

*So this is what people do when they get drunk
and pass out.*

He felt a heave come on, and he sat bolt up-
right in bed, but the wave of nausea passed.

Then the pain became more intense—the
pain in his body and in his mind.

It was like a windowsill slamming down on
his brain, over and over again. He began imagining his Honor Trial; he thought of those guys
in the dark, and then he thought of the boy who
had jumped from the tower decades ago and
wondered what that had felt like.

5

The towers were very nearly inaccessible to students, owing to the one suicide the school had
ever had.

All Jim really knew about it was that a senior
had jumped because something bad had happened in his life—drugs were the culprit according to popular lore. There was, perhaps, a
love motive, since the boy had sent a dozen red

roses to a woman in the village who was much older and perhaps even pregnant—so went the tale—and the boy left a note that mysteriously disappeared (again, the legend had grown over the years to include this detail, although no student could corroborate this wrinkle).

As a result, the entrances to the towers were locked most of the time, and only accessible with permission and when a student was accompanied by a teacher or administrator. After studying the ancient world, Fricker had begun calling them "ziggurats." Jim Hook didn't think he'd ever consider climbing them and jumping out of them.

But it was late; he couldn't sleep; his mouth tasted like rat dung; his head burst anew with stings and squeezes and a blam-blam-blam pulsing ache; Mojo was snoring in his small bed nearby, and a glow of moonlight had crept down the casement and through the sliver of open window. Jim looked out through it, and saw a bit of ziggurat reaching skyward from among the wispy trees.

He drew his gym shorts on, and scuffled into a rugby shirt that stank from need of a good washing. Feeling thirsty in a way he had never felt before, he stuck his head under the bathroom sink and gobbled down what seemed like a gallon of water before turning off the spigot and heading out. He just wanted to get out of the Trenches and the stifling, unbreathable air, away from the dreadful thoughts of what his meager future held, and out into the night.

He snuck past Bleeder's room, creaking floors and all, and when he opened the back door, he felt ice in the wind.

6

It was freezing out. The temperature had dropped so many degrees since he'd been out earlier that it was suddenly like winter. He pulled the long sleeves of the rugby shirt down over the palms of his hands, and began jogging down the flagstone path toward the road that led up to the towers.

When he reached the Great Door, he glanced back along the road to see if anyone might be there—there were at least two security guards who were supposed to be patrolling the grounds at night, but usually they were watching television in the teachers' lounge. The spotlights hit the fountain and St. George and the Dragon perfectly—the water was turned off, and the dragon looked very nearly doglike, a Doberman crossed with a goose, but with bat wings, and St. George's spear struck the beast right in its shoulder. Leaves swirled about in the wind, falling to the pavement and gravel—but no one seemed to be about.

For a moment, Jim took it all in: the night,

the waving trees, the sound of some distant bird, the feeling of absolute human aloneness in the universe. The pulsing in his head hadn't diminished with his run, but he was feeling better being out in the chill.

He went to the tower at the right hand side of the building. The door was curved in a smooth arch, and looked as medieval as a tower entrance could be. Lit by one of the stronger lights, it looked like the entrance to some Rapunzel castle.

And of course, it was locked.

Then Jim went to the tower to the left of the Great Door. The light was dim—shadows from the branches of a nearby tree flagged back and forth across the lamplight. Perhaps it was the stones of the tower itself, but this corner felt colder just stepping up to the worn stone step that led to the door. He tried the door, but it was locked as well.

"How the hell am I going to jump when I can't even get inside the damn thing?" he asked the night.

Then he sat down on the step and began weeping again, and felt like the biggest pussy in the world. The pounding hangover took over, and he began shivering from the cold.

He leaned back against the tower door, and it opened behind him.

7

Jim told himself that it wasn't just some imagined fear that held him back; nor was it the hammering in his head from his first-ever hangover; nor was it because, at this hour between night and dawn, every movement was fraught with a kind of inherent spookiness.

It was simply the darkness within the tower.

It was pitch black, and he had the terrible feeling that something stood within the small room of the tower—what would have, in another time, been considered the guard room—and that something was waiting just for him to set foot inside.

He remained outside, staring at the open door for several moments, and then pulled the door shut again.

He had no interest in exploring that place. He shivered, just thinking of it.

Jim began shambling back to the Trenches—his thirst growing immense, his stomach hurting, his head still popping and crashing, and when he reached the dorm, he turned back for a moment to look at the tower.

He thought he saw a flicker of light at one of the uppermost windows, but then, nothing.

And then he decided to go back to the tower and up those stairs.

8

He got a flashlight from his room and convinced Meloni to come along with him, mainly because he didn't want to go up there all by himself feeling half-drunk and all-scared and a little bit chickenshit. It had taken ten minutes to wake Meloni from a sound sleep, and another three to make him a cup of coffee by mixing Maxwell House instant with hot water from the tap. It tasted like dog doo, but it did the trick.

"Always wanted to go up the tower," Mojo said.

9

"Crap, look at this," Mojo Meloni said when they came around the first curved stair of the tower. "Shine the light up."

Jim shot the beam above his head. The curved steps were warped with age, and narrow.

"How many steps you think we have to climb to get to the top?"

"I dunno. It's a ways up."

"Fuck yes it's a ways up. Now, why'd I let you talk me into this?"

"Because I'm scared shitless to go up by myself."

"Face it, Hook, you're just scared shitless, pe-

211

riod. Come on. Hold the light up. I'll go first."
And Mojo went ahead, moaning now and then
about how sleepy he was and how the steps
seemed to go on forever and how it reminded
him of this campfire story about these kids who
get caught in a rainstorm and enter this castle
and start going up these stairs just like these
stairs and there are only one hundred steps, but
as they run back down they realize there are
more steps down, many more than a hundred,
and they keep going down down down.

"Thanks for that." Jim shivered. "Not like I
believe it."

"Me neither," Mojo said, but began counting
the steps aloud as he went.

10

"One hundred seventy-two," Mojo said when he
reached the top, out of breath. "Come on, Hook,
get the light up here."

Jim's limbs ached and he was breathing hard,
but he made it up the last steps. "I think my ears
just popped."

He shone the light around the small room
they now stood in. Three long windows with
shutters on the inside rounded the curve of the
tower room. Mojo went to open the one in the
middle. He drew the shutters back, latching
them in place. This brought in another glow of
light from the big lights along the drive below.

"Gotta match?" Jim asked as he directed the light's beam to the several fat candles that were on the floor.

"Always," Mojo said, reaching in the breast pocket of his T-shirt. He lit three of the candles, which lit the turret well enough to see its flickering edges. "It's like an old castle."

"Yep. Wonder why they don't let us up here."

"Jumpers."

"Jumpers?"

"Kids jump. You know, like Dutch last year, who got all suicidal when his girl dumped him and tried to slit his wrists after he had toked up too much. And that kid jumped a long time ago. I heard about it."

"It's a nice view up here," Jim said as he opened up another set of shutters.

"Looky here." Mojo walked to a low door right next to the top step. He pulled on the door and then pushed, but it wouldn't give. "I wonder where this goes to."

"Let me try," Jim said.

"Okay, Mr. Strongman."

Jim pressed on the door, and felt it give slightly. But it was definitely locked. "We could jimmy it."

"Why?" Mojo asked.

Jim shrugged.

"I got to ask you something," said Mojo.

"Shoot."

"What's going on with you?"

213

"Meaning?"

"Meaning you know what I mean."

"I'm not sure. I think I'm losing it."

"What else?"

"You mean, no one told you?" asked Jim.

"Told me what?"

"I'm going up for an honor violation."

"What?"

"I'm not supposed to talk about it."

"Aw, Hook. Man! That sucks. Want a joint?"

"Nope."

"I got one here." Mojo patted his pocket.

"No. Seriously. Thanks."

"God," Mojo said. "Life sucks." Then, "You ain't gonna jump, are you?"

Jim glanced out the open window. "Don't think so. Not right now anyway. It ain't a bad idea." He nearly laughed.

"Don't jump, that's my advice," Mojo said, as if it were perfectly reasonable advice against a perfectly reasonable decision, and then lit up his joint. "That is totally fucked-up, Hooky. Fuck this school and its fucked-up rules and regs." Distracted, Mojo began laughing. He pointed at the ceiling. "Freaky, freak. Holy shit, look at that."

Jim glanced up, but even with the candle-light, it was hard to see what Mojo was pointing at. He directed the flashlight's beam to the ceiling of the tower. Chalk drawings of skulls and crossbones and knives and something that was some kind of scraggly circle with lines around it were all over the ceiling.

Around the edge of the ceiling, the words: DON'T FUCK WITH CADAVERS.

Chapter Twenty-one
A Turn of the Screw

1

"What the *frig* is that?" Bilge asked, pointing at the gray matter on Jim's plate.

It was 7:30 A.M., and the first bell would sound in ten minutes. The dining hall was packed with students, some of whom milled about the trash cans, where everyone was whining about some midterm in Latin; others were devouring breakfasts at one lunge; and some of the upperclassmen were loading up on Coke and coffee to get a morning buzz going.

Jim Hook sat at the table across from Bilge and Tippy and Mojo, and wished he had just skipped the morning meal. Wished he had just

217

skipped waking up after four hours' sleep. Wished a lot of things. "Biscuits and gravy. Maybe some sausage."

"It's shit on a friggin' shingle," Bilge said. "It looks like . . . like . . . *diarrhea.*"

"Will someone tell Bilgebreath there's no such word as frig," Mojo said wearily.

"Yuck." Tippy pushed his plate away, and made vomiting noises.

Nick Costain, a pale blond sophomore who had transferred over from Deerfield—purportedly because of bad grades—scrambled through the dining hall bleating, "Holy crap, has anyone seen Carrington? He has my Bio notes and I need them now. Bloody hell. Bloody bloody hell." He was nearly in tears, and even some of the younger boys were snickering at him, with his tie all twisted like brambles and his hair a mess of gel and grease. "He's gonna pay, Carrington's gonna pay!"

"Damn it, Bilge, you ruined my eggs," Kip French said, covering his plate with his paper napkin.

Jim glanced down at his plate. His stomach was already heaving, and he felt as gray as the crap sitting there, swimming in grease. "Yeah, thanks, Bilge, for the image." He reached for the dry toast at the center of the table, and drew two slices over to his napkins. He drank the last of his milk, and chewed on the toast as he pushed himself up out of his chair.

Mischief

Breakfast was always hectic—the seniors didn't monitor so much as they broke up morning fights, and Ms. Fidget—real name, Fitzgerald—with her meat arms and avocado hips, sat near the entrance to the dining hall at a small folding table, sucking back coffee like it was air.

As he got just outside the dining area, feeling as if his tie were on backward, with crumbs of bread on his chin—which he swiped at with his fingers—he saw Miles, standing near the large oriel window that overlooked the soccer field. The kid was looking out the window, and the back of his head looked ragged, mainly because the lightly stained glass had cast an aura around him.

2

"Miles," Jim said, coming up to him. "What's up, kiddo? Shrike still riding your tail?"

Miles twisted his neck around to see Jim, but Jim perceived something different for a moment. It was as if someone else were standing there with Miles, not next to Miles, but specifically where Miles stood. Another boy, just about Miles's height and weight, and most of the other boy was a blur.

Man, this hangover. I will never drink a drop of liquor again in all my life. Never ever ever ever, Jim promised himself.

"Hey Hook," Miles said. "Look at this." He

motioned for him to look out the window.

Jim went over, and looked out over the arches of the abbey, across the soccer field and the scattered woods beyond. "Hey, Mole," he said, feeling warm just at the sight of the kid.

"It's something you should see," Miles said. "It's something nobody would notice until now. Now that you're here. It's weird how it happens, huh? It's like something once gets jogged in your head and then maybe later it crosses with something that happens and it's like you get struck by lightning, only you never saw the lightning. Look. Really look."

"Okay, but where? I can't see anything."

"Right here, look. Something's coming through," Miles said, but Jim couldn't see anything out in the field. Rain had just begun falling a few seconds before, and Jim noticed that the sky was beginning to turn a pasty color. "It's already started. You brought it here, you're like a key, and now it's like you woke something up."

Then, what felt like a shiver went through Jim as he stood looking at the day through the yellow-pink of the stained glass window, and it felt as if he'd pressed his hand into some kind of mud, or some dead animal lying by the roadside, or some slick wet warm . . . thing.

Something's coming through.

He had just a moment before scruffed Miles's hair, but now no one stood next to him at all.

Miles had not moved from the spot.

He was simply not there.

In his place, Jim was positive he could see something that approximated human breath on an icy day. An intense chill overcame him, and his hands became fists—his muscles tightened—against the icy sensation.

But the worst part was, it wasn't an unfamiliar feeling to him.

3

During study hall, Jim passed Trey Fricker a note:

I think I'm cracking up. I'm seeing things. Skip fourth period. Meet me out by the woods.

Fricker wrote back:

Okay. This better be good. The woods where?

Jim wrote back:

Near the boneyard.

Fricker wrote back:

Why?

Jim wrote:

It's important.

4

Jim told him everything.

They could see the graveyard from the path.

The rain had all but stopped spitting; the brilliant yellows and reds of the leaves that carpeted the woods seemed to brighten as the sun gradually came out from behind the clouds, and Jim told him about the students who had grabbed him, the finger with the ring, and Miles, who had faded into the stained glass window.

"Miles who?" Fricker asked.

"The kid from seventh grade. Only I find out this morning from Mrs. Boone, there's no Miles in seventh grade. There's no Miles in the school. There's no Miles anywhere."

"Miles to go before I sleep," Fricker said.

"Huh?"

"Nothing. Just thinking out loud."

Jim didn't stop with Miles; he went on and on about the tower and the door opening; the feeling of being watched constantly; the sense that something terrible was about to happen.

"So, what you're saying is, you're losing it."

Jim laughed out loud. "Yeah. Yeah! That's what I'm saying," he said, clapping his hands together. "Man, that feels good."

"Well, Jim, my man, you are losing it, but good." They walked along together, smushing mud and crunching through leaves that had escaped the rainfall. "It sounds like it's maybe all this shit from the Honor Trial."

"I didn't make it up. All of it. The stuff about the other students. They pretty much beat the crap out of me."

"Okay, I'll accept that as fact. So there's some

secret group of guys who have some club. Like the Key Club only . . . evil." Fricker giggled. "Sorry, man." He drew a pack of smokes from his pocket and lit one up. "You been getting high these last couple days?"

"Nope."

Fricker sucked on the cigarette like it was a breast. "All right. So let's assume it all happened."

"I mean, it did," Jim said.

"Maybe you *should* get high. Want to get high?"

Jim shook his head. "No."

"We could go to the bongatorium and light up with the stoners, and then maybe you'd get more lucid about all this. Or at least not look like you were going to jump off a cliff."

"I look like that?"

Fricker grinned. "Oh yeah, buddy. You look like that. Like you're going to jump off the highest cliff in all of Christendom."

"And the finger."

"You still got it?"

"I stuck it in my dresser."

"Kee-rist."

"And that whole story about Stephen and my dad."

"Well, that's no doubt pure crap. If there is some little secret clique here, they're probably just playing off all those stories about that shit."

"About my dad?" Jim asked. He stopped. The

silence of the woods overcame him. He felt as if the world had somehow stopped spinning. "There are stories about my dad?"

"Not really just your dad. Both of them," Fricker said matter-of-factly.

"Like what?"

"What, you never heard them?"

"Never."

"It was some senior. Last year. He had known your brother when this guy was a freshman. They were pretty good friends. When your brother got killed in that wreck, he had this story that sort of spread that your brother and your dad were at some whorehouse down in the city. That's all."

"That's *all*?"

"Oh, come on. Come on, Hook. You musta heard all that before. Someone musta told you."

Jim blurted, "It was a car wreck. The other guy—driving the other car—was drinking."

"What other guy? Hook, there was no other guy. Your dad was drunk. Everyone knows it. Everyone but you."

That's when Jim balled up his fist and swung a punch without even realizing he'd raised his arm.

5

Got Trey Fricker right beneath the jaw, too, and practically knocked the cigarette right out of his hand, but Fricker managed to move with the punch and keep his balance.

"My dad wasn't drunk, that's a goddamn lie!" Jim shouted, standing there, his fist in the air ready for another swing.

"Batshit, Hook, calm down," Fricker said out of the side of his mouth, cig thrust between his lips. He reached up and rubbed his chin. "Owie, that hurt."

"Take it back."

Fricker looked at him defiantly. "No. The truth is the truth. To . . . to deny it would be like another honor violation, Hook, and you know it. Face it."

Jim spat at his feet. "I thought you were my friend."

"I am," Fricker said. "Keep your damn temper, dude."

Jim felt so much better from the hit, even though his fist was aching like a son of a bitch, that he wasn't even all that mad at Fricker. "It's just a lie someone made up somewhere. I am so sick of everybody telling lies."

"You're so sick of 'em you're willing to tell a few yourself, right?" Fricker said. He looked like a strange sort of philosopher with the cig hanging from his mouth, his hair a mess, his chin already bruising a little. "Hey, I got a joke. Listen up. A guy is really horny and he goes to this whorehouse. He says, 'I gotta get me a girl.' The madam shouts up the stairs, 'Hey, Joe, get

Betty down here!' The guy says, 'How much is Betty?' And the madam says, 'A hundred bucks.' 'Well,' says the guy, 'I can't afford her.' 'Okay,' the madam says. Then she shouts up the stairs, 'Hey, Joe, send down Bertha!' and the guy says, 'How much is Bertha?' and the madam says, 'Twenty bucks.' And the guy says, 'Aw, I can't afford her. Got anyone cheaper?' The madam says, 'So how much you got?' and the guy says, 'Two bucks,' and the madam shouts up the stairs, 'Hey, Joe! Grease up the cat!'"

"Why'd you tell me that stupid joke?" Jim asked, but he had to crack a smile. It was an old joke, but the way Fricker had told it, it was as bad as it had ever been.

"So's you'd laugh," Fricker said. "Why else do people tell jokes? Christ, Hook, you're seeing things, you're hungover, you're headed for an honor trial, you're in a freakin' shithole of a situation, but you still gotta laugh at jokes now and then. Even dumb ones."

6

After a few awkward minutes, they went to sit on a large rock that overlooked the Hudson River.

Jim hadn't said anything, and although thoughts formed in his mind—all causing him further headaches—he didn't want to express any of them.

Finally, on his third smoke, Fricker said, "Here's the thing, Hook. What you're going through may not be so incredible, and you may not be losing your mind. When I first came here—in seventh grade—from Parham over in Hanover, I was pretty much lost. Just like you are right now. Just like it. I was screwed up about some things and I was getting into trouble, and basically," and here he took a long suck of smoke into his lungs and then blew it all out in one great gust, "lying my way through stuff. I wasn't quite together yet. Harrow's hard on guys. We all know it. We know that getting through classes and making the grade here is like rope-climbing with greasy palms. Maybe, just maybe, whoever these guys are, they're trying to make your life easier. Maybe they can take care of this whole honor violation thing for you. Or maybe it's a test. Maybe it's the Honor Council testing to see if you'll cheat further. All kinds of crap goes on here that's confusing. There's one group I heard of that sounds like the one who got to you."

Jim looked at him. "Who are they?"

Fricker shrugged. "They're called the Cadaver something." He spoke as if this were a sacred utterance. As if, just by saying it, something uninvited had arrived.

"You hear things sometimes about them. They're around. They may just be seniors. Maybe they're juniors and sophomores, too.

They're secret. Okay, I knew this one kid. He was in trouble, and suddenly he was getting good grades, or things were sort of going his way, and I asked him about it and he said it was nothing. Then one day in the showers, I noticed this thing—on his butt."

Fricker grinned. "Right on his cheek. It was like a smiley face, and I told him, and he told me to shut the fuck up. Now this guy was kind of a friend of mine up until then, and later on I'm thinking it's not a smiley face on his ass, but a big C. So I'm talking to these three guys when we go down to St. Cat's one time. This senior named Spencer is driving us, and this guy I know's name comes up and I talk about the big C on his butt, and the other guys who are passing around a joint in the backseat start cracking up, but Spencer doesn't crack a smile. Later on, when we park the car, and the stoners are off to see their stonettes, Spence pulls me aside and he tells me to stay away from this friend of mine with the C on his butt. I ask him why, and he tells me this whole long story about how his cousin used to have that C on his butt, too, and his cousin ended up transferring out of Harrow and going to Exeter to finish up, only he never finished up, he just sort of vanished, and showed up two years later in Boston all paranoid because he said someone named the Cadaver Club or something was after him and was going to kill him. So I don't think much of this, but when when I hear from this guy Spence again, he's graduating last year, and it's almost graduation time, and he tells me something else about this. He tells me they're after him. I ask him what he means. He tells me the Cadavers are after him and they're not going to stop until they get him. I ask him what can they do? And he says nothing then, 'cause all these other guys pour into the hall around us, but the next thing I hear is that Spence doesn't graduate. He gets caught for some honor violation and he's booted—two weeks before he'd have his diploma. Harvard went out the window. I never heard from him again, but that name kept sticking in my mind. The Cadaver Society. It's some mindfuck group, far as I can tell."

"Just my luck," Jim said.

"I had one other run-in with them," Fricker added.

"When?"

"When I was initiated," Trey Fricker said, and stubbed his cigarette out against the rock.

Chapter Twenty-two
Fricker, and a Trip to New York

1

Jim sat there, and began laughing.

Fricker looked at him funny. "What the hell are you laughing about?"

"Right. You're one of them. It can't be real. It's all a joke, right? A big setup for a prank?"

"It's real," Fricker said, and the ensuing silence was like a gag over Jim's mouth again. He struggled to say something, but nothing occurred to him. So many things welled up in Jim at the moment that he got just what Fricker was saying, that it took a few seconds before he shoved him hard, and Fricker fell back in the muddy grass.

Douglas Clegg

Fricker just sat there, shaking his head. "That make you feel better?"

"Sure did."

All Jim could think about were the things those guys had told him in the dark, how they'd hit him, how they knew things about his mother and said terrible things about his father and brother.

There was a vibe he was picking up from Fricker—something that both scared him a little and intrigued him a lot. What was it that Fricker knew? If he knew this kind of stuff about his life, what did he know from this sinister society about other kids? And maybe they weren't all that bad. Maybe they really wanted to help him keep his scholarship and stay at Harrow.

Some small part of him fought against this. It seemed wrong. It all seemed wrong. Better to just go to Trimalchio and admit what he did, get booted, go back to Yonkers, go to a regular school without all these rich kids, and work hard.

But all he could see was his brother. Stephen. The words forming in his mind.

How you gonna make your big bro proud?

2

"What the hell is it all about?" Jim asked, calming only slightly.

232

"I can't tell you anything else. I'd be in trouble for telling you what I just told you. But I trust you. We're friends, right?"

"Who's in the Cadavers?"

"I can't tell you. I don't even know everybody."

"What the fuck does that mean?"

"Look, we're told where and when. We get there, it's dark. I mean, I've seen a couple guys. But not all seven of them."

"Seven?"

"Yeah. There can only be seven. There are six right now. You'll complete the group."

"How did—were you part of finding out about my mom? Did you go—go through her things?"

"No. And that's enough. Friends or not, if you ask me anything else, so help me God, Hook, I will tell them to back off and you will be thrown out on your ass in an Honor Trial."

"All right. I need your help then."

"Okay."

"I need to get to the city. I need to find out about the woman. Ivy Martin."

"Part of the rules, Hook: I can't help you. Not one bit. This is your test, not mine."

"I don't have even a way to get down there."

"Sorry."

"Thanks," Jim spat. "Some friend you are."

"You want to know what kind of friend I am, Jim? I'll tell you. I'm the kind that did not want you to get kicked out on your ass for some stupid interpretation of this honor code because Kelleher has it out for you—which he does—or because assholes like Hugh Carrington, who cheats half the time himself, noticed that you looked at my paper a couple of times. But the biggest problem here, Hook, is that you did look at my paper. Didn't you? You did. You broke the code. And you can either fall for it or you can get around it. Don't be stupid. Not now. Seriously, man. I've known you long enough to know what you want more than anything, and it ain't getting kicked out of here on your ass and going back to Yonkers." He emphasized *Yonkers* like it was another word for *shit*.

"Nothin' wrong with Yonkers."

"Whatever."

"Go to hell," Jim said, flipping the bird as he stomped off.

Trey Fricker called after him, "And don't go blabbing this to anyone, Hook, I mean it. You talk about this—we even suspect you talk—and it's over for you!"

3

"All right. I've thought about it," Jim said. It was after supper, and he'd caught up with Fricker out on the track. Trey Fricker had on his gym shorts and a T-shirt, and Jim wore his sweats. They jogged side by side for a while in silence.

"It's serious shit," Fricker said as he ran. "Don't let us down."

"What about that finger?"

"Don't ask me anything." Fricker pumped his arms up and down with his breathing. "I told you not to. Don't break the rules here."

"All right," Jim huffed, having to run a little faster to keep up. "All right."

They jogged another lap, Fricker getting several feet ahead. Then, coming around the curve of the track, Jim caught up again.

"I just need to find out about this Blue Glass place and Ivy Martin, right?"

Fricker said nothing.

"And something she's got."

"Stolen. Your brother stole it. She has it. Get it." Fricker took off at a sprint, and Jim slowed to a walk.

Darkness surrounded the the track, which was lit bright as day.

Afterward, they both sat in the bleachers while Fricker lit up a cig. They didn't say anything, and Jim wasn't feeling anything other than sleepy.

He was going to give in.

The questions in his head were too much.

He wanted to know who the hell Ivy Martin was, and if she was his father's whore, why his father and Stephen had both gone down to New York City that night, and why they both ended up dead.

And he wanted to get into this secret club now more than anything.

He wanted to know exactly who he needed to hate the most.

4

Jim Hook slept the best he had in days that night, falling into bed by nine P.M., and even his dreams seemed blank and black and empty and unmemorable.

He awoke on Thursday feeling pretty damn good.

It wasn't until third period that someone started talking about how Hugh Carrington was now officially missing, and everyone thought that he'd run off because they found a letter in his room that talked about how he was in love with another boy and couldn't live with this kind of shame anymore.

But Jim knew who had gotten Carrington out of the way. He didn't know how they did it.

Something pressed into him—a palpable pressure along his spine.

He had to tell someone.

He had to talk to someone.

5

On the pay phone at the library:

"Can you come over tonight?"

"Jim? Tonight? I don't know. I'll be there to-morrow night."

"It's got to be tonight. It's hard for me to ex-plain. But I need your help. Can you get Jenny's car?"

"Is it that important?"

He was silent for a moment.

"Lark?"

"Still here."

He wanted to cry. Like a baby. Like a two-year-old sitting in wet diapers. But he couldn't. He didn't want to be weak through this. When he thought of his brother, he thought of how Stephen would handle this. How he would get through it. It would be all right, somehow. It would turn out just fine if he held on and made it through these hoops.

Finally, he said, "You ever need help on some-thing that was so important but you couldn't really trust anyone to talk about it with, only there was one person in the whole world you trusted and you needed their help even if you can't tell them why you need it so badly?" Was he making any sense? He didn't feel like he was.

He heard her take a breath. "All right. I'll be there. After Field Hockey. I should be there by four-thirty."

6

He waited out behind the boxwoods just be-yond the front gate. Jenny's car was an '87 Mustang that coughed black smoke as it came up the road. He stepped out of the hedge as soon as he saw it, and waved. Jenny was driving, her face red from the wind, and her smile infectious. Lark sat next to her.

Lark opened her door and Jim managed to scooch in back.

7

"We gotta get gas," Jenny said. "Who's chipping in?"

Jim was reluctant to say anything. He passed a five-dollar bill up front.

"Oh, save that, Jim," Lark said, and reached into her purse and brought out a twenty. "Here ya go."

"I can pay five bucks," Jim insisted, passing the bill up to the front seat.

Lark leaned back. "No kiss?"

He leaned forward and they shared a brief kiss.

"Hubba hubba," Jenny said. "Okay, where's the friggin' Shell station in this town?"

"There's a Mobil two blocks up, just before the highway," Jim said.

"I'm using Daddy's Shell card."

"Then why are we paying? Jenny, you sneak," Lark said.

"Pocket change for me. Now, Jim, what's so bleeding important that your main squeeze and me had to get up here so fast?" Jenny took the curve onto Main Street like she was driving for the Indy 500; black smoke came out of the back of the Mustang.

"It's kind of private," Jim replied.

"Woo." Jenny glanced at him in the rearview mirror. *"Okay."*

Lark brought her hand around to his knee. He took her hand in his.

"And where's this bitch?" Jenny said, giggling.

"Jenny!" Lark laughed, and then said, "The puppy, Jim. We figured we'd swing by and pick it up."

8

Within twenty minutes, they were on the road out of town, gassed up, and Jim held the yellow lab puppy in his lap. Its right paw was swathed in a stinky bandage. It looked up at Jim like it was looking for its mother's nipple. "I think it's farting. Phew. What if it pees?"

"Puppy pee doesn't count," Jenny said, laughing so hard she started snorting. "If it starts whining, I'll pull over and we'll let her do her business. So, we go all the way down to the Westside Highway, right? And then what?"

"I need to find a place called the Blue Glass something. It's a bar or something I think."

Jenny quickly glanced at Lark, and Lark did

239

a double take. They both guffawed at the same time.

"It's a coffeehouse, Jim."

"Yeah, we used to go there—back when *someone* we all know was seeing someone *else* we all used to know," Jenny added. She glanced at Jim in the mirror and pumped her eyebrows like Groucho Marx. "Well, I'm up for a good caffeine buzz tonight."

"Oh. I thought it would be something . . ." Jim began. "Some kind of bad place."

"Bad coffee sometimes!" Jenny practically belched a laugh.

"Pass me the puppy," Lark said. "I want to cuddle her."

He passed the whimpering dog to the front seat, where it took up half of Lark's lap.

"This is the cutest puppy I've ever seen." Lark brought the ball of fur and drool up to her face and kissed it all over its ears and neck; the puppy, in turn, began licking her nose.

"Griselda," Jenny said.

"Griselda?"

"The name. Or Marti. That's a good name for a bitch."

"I don't think we should name it if we have to give it up," Jim said.

"Why not keep it?" Jenny said, rolling her window down and letting the nearly icy air brush through the car briefly before sending the

window back up. "You could take it home this
weekend."

"I don't want to go home this weekend," Lark
said.

"Well, Jim, what about you? You could take
it home. Does your dad want a dog?"

"Jen."

"My father's dead," Jim said, glancing out the
window at the dark interrupted by brief lights
off the road, through the windswept trees.

"Oops. Sorry. Me and my big mouth." Jenny
gave Lark a look that must've meant *You never
tell me anything*.

"My mom's allergic to most animals, anyway," Jim said, an afterthought.

Silence ruled the car then, until Jenny
reached across and popped open the glove com-
partment. "Pass me that CD, the one on top,"
she motioned to Lark.

Lark opened the CD case, and handed the
disc to Jenny. Seconds later, Alanis Morissette
was singing, and the volume was pumped up,
and the puppy began barking.

Jenny was a bit of a freak for speed, and it
surprised Jim how quickly they were on the
Westside Highway almost into the city, doing a
lot of offensive driving past and between the
slower-moving vehicles. He checked his seat
belt two or three times to make sure it would
hold, and every now and then he saw some angry motorist near them give Jenny the finger as

she maneuvered the Mustang between lanes.

Rain began drizzling; the windshield wipers screeched at first as they started their metronome beat; the CD had finished playing; and Lark said, suddenly, "Jen, next light, next light—take it. We can take it to Ninth and then turn back to get there."

As Jenny brought the car to a screeching halt at the light, she said, "Tell me again, Jim. Who are ya looking for at the Blue Glass?"

"My dad's whore," he said.

Chapter Twenty-three
The Blue Glass

1

The Blue Glass was crushed between two large shops—one a costume shop, its windows packed with masks of goblins and witches for Halloween; the other, a sex shop, with whips and whipped cream and porn magazines in its display.

The coffee house had a narrow doorway; above it, a large round blue glass globe in a net. When Jim, carrying the pup, whom they were now calling Alanis, stepped inside, the smell of incense mixed with tobacco was overpowering, and even the dog coughed at first. They walked down the steps to the sunken room; several round tables were spread across a narrow room that seemed to stretch deep into the building that housed it. Along the back wall, a bar where the coffee and pastries were served; and a stage so small it was barely more than another table.

Sitting on the table, a magician doing some kind of card trick for a small group of less-than-interesteds who were downing espresso and iced coffees like there was not caffeine enough in the world to satisfy them.

Jim had just about enough cash to cover this. "Two cappuccinos."

"Coming right up."

"This the only Blue Glass in the city?"

The man behind the counter nodded. "Far as we can tell."

Jim didn't hesitate. "I'm looking for someone named Ivy. Ivy Martin."

The man nodded. "Sure. She's upstairs."

"Upstairs?"

"I only manage here. Miss Martin owns the place. Does she know you?" The man reached for the phone beneath the counter, bringing it up. "I'll ring her up if you like."

"I think . . . she and my dad were friends. The name's Hook."

"Hook," the man said and then dialed a number and whispered into the phone. Then he handed Jim a key.

2

Jim brought the large cups brimming with white foam to the table. Lark was still cooing over the puppy.

"I don't get it," Jenny said, grabbing her cup as if it contained holy water. She took a big sip and ended up with a white mustache on her upper lip. "What's the big mystery we're too stupid to be told about?"

"It's nothing," Jim said. "Honest. I just need to check something out. The woman who owns this place knew my dad."

"Yeah, his whore. Right. So, what, you're going to confront her or something?" Jenny asked.

"I guess I just need to know for sure," Jim said.

"Use me for my wheels, will you?" Jen said, half joking.

"I'm sorry," Jim said.

"Go do what you need to do, Jim," Lark said. "We'll wait here."

3

Jim had to go around the back of the building, down a narrow alleyway, to get to the door. He used the key the guy at the counter had given him, unlocked the door, and saw a long rickety staircase up.

Trash lined the stairs; the banister was wobbly; each time he took a step he heard a massive creak and was sure that at any moment, he would plunge through the cheap, ancient wood. But he made it up to the single apartment on the landing.

He pressed the buzzer. Waited. Pressed it again.

The door opened slightly.

"You're his brother?" the woman said. "Of course you are. You look just like him. It's like . . . it's like seeing him again." A smile lit up her face, and she opened the door wider to let him in.

4

The inside of the apartment was nothing like the stairs up to it. It was a huge loft space with a spiral staircase up to a small room above, and what looked like a full kitchen in another room. The furnishings were old and quite beautiful; some kind of Japanese lantern hung in the middle of the room, a great white light; and the room itself seemed to emanate warmth and coziness. Jim glanced around at the overstuffed chairs and the great peacock pattern wall hanging, and the windows that looked out over all the buildings until the Hudson River came into view.

It was not quite the whorehouse he had expected.

And she was not what he had expected, either.

Ivy Martin was in her mid-twenties, and looked sleek and refined. Her golden hair was pulled back away from a face that could have adorned a Calvin Klein ad—she was a thoroughbred of a woman, bringing with it all the notions of horses and beauty and money. She was not some whore, he could tell that right off—or if she was, she was one of the most successful whores in all of Christendom, as Fricker would say.

"We finally meet," she said, extending her hand; she had a firm handshake. Something in her manner seemed overeager; her eyes sparkled as if she had just discovered something new and exciting. "Would you like something to drink? Coffee? A Coke?"

"Sure. Coke. Thanks."

"Have a seat," she said, and finally he detected some degree of nervousness in her voice. She had a funny gait as she walked—as if she were disguising a slight limp. She was one of the most sophisticated and beautiful women he had ever seen. She almost reminded him of that picture in a book he'd seen the other day. Isis Something. Isis with her calamitous beauty. Ivy had that, too. She was calamitous in her beauty.

He sat down on a large sofa that seemed

decadent with its enormous cushions and large back—it farted when he sat down on it, and he made the noise twice more to reassure himself that it was the sofa and not him. She came back in with two glasses of soda, and set them down on the coffee table in front of him. Then she took the spindly chair across from him.

"I assume you've come about your brother."

"I guess. I guess I'm not sure why I came."

"Well, I always heard about you. Are you all right? You look a little pale."

"I'm always pale," Jim said, and then she laughed slightly. It was an adorable laugh.

Christ, what was he going to say to her? He glanced around the walls—paintings of what he imagined were European gardens and lakes hung haphazardly as if she had just liked one or the other of them, and put them up as she bought them. Three doors near the kitchen—other rooms. And of course he knew: She wasn't anyone's whore. She wasn't anything to stick a label on.

She was Ivy Martin, and the Cadavers didn't know everything. They didn't really know what had gone on here with this woman and his father and his brother. They knew a little bit, and they made the rest up.

They were liars.

Why was he here at all?

He couldn't fathom it. "So, you know they're dead?"

The smile faded from Ivy Martin's face. "Of course I do." And then she added, an afterthought, "I was with them that night."

Jim held his breath for a few moments. He felt the room spinning.

"I want to know everything," he said.

And she told him.

5

"Your brother and I met at a party at Vassar. He was pretending to be a freshman at Harvard, and I was just pretending to be happy at a party which was less than fun. I was a senior then. We drove out of Poughkeepsie and spent the whole night talking and laughing, and then I knew that I was in love so that—even though he had to confess he was a senior in high school—it didn't really bother me, and we began seeing each other," she said, taking a sip of her soda, leaning back against the creaking chair. "It was only when he proposed that your father got involved."

"You and Stephen?"

"What did you think?"

"I guess what I think doesn't matter."

"Well, it was a whirlwind, but love can go that way, and maybe it was going to be the dumbest decision either of us had ever made. We set a date, he got me a beautiful ring, and then your

Douglas Clegg

father was having none of it. Your father tried to buy me off, which was pretty disgusting. I have always worked my way through things and have never let anyone buy me. All right, you may think I have lots of money—I went to an expensive school, I have this nice place, and yes, I'm successful at what I do, successful enough to have bought the little coffeehouse downstairs—but I work long hours and apply everything I have to my work, so it's not like I've been handed things. I only bought the Blue Glass because of Stephen. It was our favorite place."

"I don't understand. You and Stephen?"

"We dated for a year, but we just couldn't wait. Something was going on between Stephen and your—well, it's old history. It's not important. Your father was, I'm sure, a good man. He just didn't want his son to marry this soon and throw away the future. He was probably right, but there was something special about Stephen. Something—as if he—"

"As if anything he touched would turn to gold," Jim said sadly.

"Yes. Exactly. He was special, there was no doubt about it. But toward the end, he was involved in something. Some kind of group. It bothered him and he wouldn't tell me everything. He was getting a little paranoid. Look, this is a lot to hear. You were close to him, I know. He talked about you endlessly, how funny you were, how smart, how you did all

250

these creative things, how you went jogging with him, how you went on his very first date. I felt you were almost competition—but in a good way. And then," she said, "I found out I was pregnant. And everything accelerated. Including how your dad felt."

And then she told the rest, and Jim Hook listened, his knees shaking a little, the Coke tasting like sweet broken glass in his throat, and he didn't say another word until he rose to leave, an hour later.

"I don't know what to say," he said.

"Look, there's something I want you to have. I don't need it. I have other keepsakes." Ivy went over to a desk up against one of the large windows, and opened the top drawer. She brought something out, cupped in her hand.

When she handed it to him, he felt cold metal.

"He gave it to me. But I guess it's an heirloom. I think you should have it," she said.

In his hand, a ring with a reddish-purple gem at its center that seemed to change color in the light. The gem was set in the center of what looked like an oval, with a stem coming from its bottom. For a moment, he thought he'd seen it somewhere—a photo? Or a painting?

"It's an Alexandrite. They're rare. From Russia, I'd guess. It must've been your grandmother's. In daylight, it looks green," she said, almost wearily. "He told me it stood for eternal life—the shape. It's called something. He would know what it was. I'll miss this little ring. It reminds me of him. I know he'd have wanted you to have it."

Jim looked into her eyes, and when he saw tears he stepped forward, unthinking, and embraced her.

"Thank you," he said.

As Jim held her, she whispered to him, "Sometimes I think life is just a tragedy that we know is out there in the world avoiding us, and still we hunt it down until it's our own secret tragedy."

6

When he got back down to the Blue Glass, Lark was using some napkins to wipe up an area where the puppy had peed beside their table, and Jenny nursed her third cappuccino.

Lark glanced up when she saw him. "Everything okay?"

"Yeah," he said, feeling completely exhausted.

"Good," Jenny said testily, foam still on her upper lip. "Because I'm wired. If I sit here another ten minutes I'll be certifiable. And I still need to get Geometry done or I'm screwed tomorrow."

7

Lark and Jim sat in the backseat together, the puppy curling up in Jim's lap and snoring lightly. The whole trip back, Jenny talked a mile a minute and Jim whispered to Lark that he'd tell her everything soon, but that it was about his brother and it wasn't bad.

It wasn't bad at all.

8

Jim kissed her goodbye, turned away, heard the Mustang driven by the hyped-up Jenny burn rubber and spit gravel as it took off down the road.

Jim marched wearily up the drive to the school; it was only ten-thirty. He could get to his room and get at least an hour in on home-work, and then crash into blissful sleep, know-ing that his family was fairly clean of the charges brought by the Cadavers. And if the story of his father and his mythical whore were fake, then maybe, just maybe, the rest of the stories were fake, too. His father had not been seeing some whore. His brother and father were not drunk that night.

All lies.

Trey Fricker and the Cadavers had made it all up in their dark room interrogation.

He saw someone sitting up around the rim of

the St. George–and-Dragon fountain, and knew before he got there that it was the headmaster, and that this was perhaps some fresh hell awaiting him.

Chapter Twenty-four
Back to Campus

1

"Mr. Hook," Trimalchio said. He wore a heavy tweed overcoat and a bright yellow sweater that made him look sulfurous under the lights. His grin brightened when Jim reached the fountain. "You could've avoided me and gone straight to the Trenches."

"I figured you'd probably catch me one way or another."

The man put his finger up to his lips, an annoying gesture that reminded Jim of the teacher he most despised, Mr. Kelleher with his mannerisms. Trimalchio scratched at his chin. He had a five o'clock shadow made worse by the shadows of night. "I was getting some last-minute paperwork done, going over a few things, and I was thinking about you and your situation."

"Yes, sir."

Trimalchio chuckled. "Yes, sir, no, sir—whenever you boys say it, I can hear the fear. In some ways you remind me of myself when I was here at the academy, Hook. I was a scholarship student, too, and I wanted, more than anything else, to prove to myself and the world that I could get through this school, that I could be the best, that I could stand head and shoulders with the smartest and the richest and be just as they were."

Jim felt the pull of gravity; his shoulder seemed to bear a heavy weight; he was tired and knew that bad things were on their way to him like nails to a coffin. "I'm in trouble, aren't I, sir?"

"Hear me out, Hook. I worked very hard. Do you know the Rudyard Kipling poem, 'If'?"

"No, sir."

"Here." Trimalchio patted the edge of the fountain. "Sit down. All right? I'm not going to slice you from nave to chops like Chambers would."

Jim sat beside him, and shivered. His sweater wasn't enough to keep out the chill he was feeling.

"You should commit this poem to memory. I

did, when I was here. I believe it. It's about arriving at manhood. I remember your brother, when he was here. And I see you." Trimalchio reached over and scruffed up Jim's hair. Jim didn't like touchy-feely stuff from teachers. It meant bad things for you when they broke personal space. It meant they had no problem telling you something difficult and mean to your face. He was prepared.

Trimalchio continued: "And you're not your brother."

Jim hung his head slightly. "I know, sir. I probably never will be."

"Your brother," Trimalchio began, "was a good soldier, by Harrow standards. He got the grades, he balanced the sports with social life, he excelled in ways that were noticeable. I was thinking about all this, tonight, about how you and he and I . . . what do you believe in, Hook?"

"Sir?"

Trimalchio motioned with his hands like they were rolling over each other. "Believe as in what do you in your core believe about school, about learning, about what you go through from boy to man?"

"I guess . . . I don't know."

"Know."

"Sir?"

"Know. Right now, know what it is you believe."

"I'm going to be thrown out, aren't I?" Jim

looked at him from the corner of his eyes. Trimalchio was a decent headmaster most of the time, and some of the boys even admired him. But Jim felt like the man was a frustrated something—that he wanted to do something else with his life but had been pulled back into Harrow at some point and could not get out to save his life. He knew that all of his own life was wrapped up in this guy's hands. Nave to chops, that's what Old Man Chambers called it when one of the boys was getting punishment. *We're going to slice you from nave to chops for this*, Chambers would say.

And that was what awaited Jim, no matter how nicely Trimalchio put it. *You could sweeten up the words, but in the end, it was nave to chops, and you spilled your guts and then the 'Row had you*.

"You are in violation right now," Trimalchio said softly. "You aren't to leave campus, particularly midweek, but particularly now. You know that, don't you?"

Jim nodded.

Trimalchio brought out his pipe, which was always with him, it seemed. He lit it, and puffed away. The chilly air became laced with some sweet cherry tobacco. "When I was your age, here, I had a really good friend. We were practically brothers. Best friends. But I didn't know what was going on in his mind. Not when I needed to. He killed himself, Hook. Right here on campus. He had been caught stealing something, and he had gone before the Honor Council, and he was getting booted. His parents were going to pick him up the following morning. Instead, he was dead."

"I'm sorry. That's awful."

"It was," Trimalchio said, and put his hand on Jim's shoulder. "Here's the thing, Hook. I believed he was innocent of the charges brought against him. I may have been wrong. But I believed this system failed him. This honor code that doesn't take the inner workings of human beings into consideration." He paused, and drew his pipe from his mouth, cupping it like a bird in his hand. "Did you cheat?"

"I—"

"Don't answer. I actually don't care. What I care about is, are you sorry for what happened?"

"Very."

"Good. I assume you were off doing something of importance tonight?"

"Yes, sir. Extremely."

"All right. I'll overlook this," Trimalchio said, pressing the pipe back between his lips, nodding. "As I said before, I was looking over your papers earlier this evening. You should be doing better in your classes. You should be enjoying life here more. This incident should never have happened. What I find is the missing ingredient of self-knowledge, Hook. Who are you?

Douglas Clegg

Do you know? What do you believe? To what
tenets of faith do you subscribe? What will best
allow you to grow in whatever time you have
here?"

Jim wasn't sure how to respond. They all
sounded like trick questions.

"All I know . . ." he began. "All I know is I
want to make my brother proud of me. For his
memory." He felt embarrassed to say it aloud,
as if he'd taken off all his clothes right there,
and once and for all told the world that yes, his
dick was small, his brain was fried, and his shit
stank. That's what it felt like. He felt his face
turn red.

"That's all right," Trimalchio said. "You
know, the night my friend died—killed himself
here—I thought he was trying to tell me something earlier. Something about Harrow. Not
about what he'd been accused of, but something
he believed. I'll never know what it was. He
died. It was over." A wind rushed down through
the trees, brushing brown and yellow leaves
down into the lights, and sending an arctic chill
through them. "It's nearly November. It's going
to be freezing in a day or two."

"Yes, sir."

Trimalchio took a deep breath. "You can't
take back the past and shine it up so it's all better. You just can't. Go on to your room. Tell the
housemaster or your R.A. or whoever crosses
you that you have had my permission to be out

260

tonight. That I am aware of it. I'll back it up."

"But . . . sir? Wouldn't that be a violation?"

"Hook?" Trimalchio chuckled. "Good lord, no. It's me giving you permission."

Trimalchio looked up to the trees and the flickering starlight. "We're so small here, Hook. Our concerns. Our divisions. Tonight you're worried about an Honor Trial, but trust me, regardless of the outcome, those stars will still be there tomorrow night and the night after. And in a few weeks, or a few months, this will seem like indigestion for you, or the memory of a bad dream, or nothing at all. So, promise me, no leaping off buildings or stepping into nooses, all right?"

"Yes, sir."

"Good. And don't forget to read the Kipling. Take it to heart. Oh, and Hook, one more thing."

"Sir?"

"Do you think any of the other students are pranksters?"

Jim wanted to say, "Sir?" again, but it would sound goofy. He shrugged.

"Pranks. Practical jokes. Like that Crown boy used to do last year. Do you think we have pranksters here?"

"Maybe. It depends. What kind of pranks?"

Trimalchio shrugged, looking off in the distance, distracted. "Oh, perhaps email pranks. Phone calls. That sort of thing."

"I don't know, sir."

"All right. Thanks. Goodnight, Hook. Get back to your room now."

Jim nodded, feeling a surge of elation that he wasn't going to get into trouble after all, and began walking across the gravel path toward the Trenches.

2

The first thing he did when he got to his room—Mojo on the headphones tapping on his laptop—was to go looking for the finger. It wasn't there, although a small bloodstain remained in a corner of his dresser.

"Hey, Mojo," he said, pulling the headphones off his roommate's ears. "Did you go through my drawers?"

"What the fuck?" Mojo said. Then added, "Don't be absurd."

Jim felt blood pump through his system in a way he hadn't felt before—ever. He felt victorious. "Okay. Look, I need to go out."

"Man, Trimalchio and Angstrom both were looking for you before. I think maybe you need to stay put."

"It'll be all right. Just cover for me, okay? I've got permission from Trimalchio himself. That's all anyone needs to know if they come looking for me."

3

"Get up," Jim whispered in the dark.

Then he flicked the light up.

Trey Fricker sat up. "What the—"

"I got what you wanted. What they wanted. Now, I want to know more." Jim held up Ivy Martin's ring. "This it?"

Fricker rolled out of bed, crawling to the nightstand for his cigarettes. He had one lit and in his mouth before he said another word. "Christ, Hook."

His roommate, Shep Shepard, sat up in bed. Shep was squirrelly and geeky and quiet, and Jim hadn't really noticed him all that much in the past. But Shep was up in no time, and grabbed his glasses. "Shit, he got it," Shep said.

"Shut up," Fricker said. "Get on the horn and tell them emergency powwow." He drew something out of the nightstand drawer, and stood up. "Get over here, Hook."

"Why?" Jim looked from Fricker to Shep, and then suddenly wished he hadn't barged in with the ring.

"I said so. You want in, you want protection, you want it all, you do as I say. Get over here *now*, Hook."

Jim went to him, and Fricker said, "Open your mouth and close your eyes and you will get a big surprise."

"Yeah, right."

"Just do it."

Jim shut his eyes and opened his mouth. Fricker put some kind of pill on his tongue. Then Fricker handed him a glass of water.

"Drink it down like a good boy."

"What is it?"

"It ain't Vitamin C, that's for fuckin' sure," Fricker said. "Swallow it."

"Trying to kill me?"

"No," Fricker said. "To save you. Don't worry, Hook. It's okay. Trust me on this."

You're a damn idiot and you give in to peer pressure too easily, Jim told himself, but took a sip. He opened his eyes, trying to figure out a way to spit the pill out, but it went down his gullet. *Shit*.

And it wasn't water he'd been given. It might've been vodka or grain alcohol. He couldn't tell.

"It's only a roofie cocktail," Shep said, covering up the cell phone speaker with his hand.

"Jesus," Jim said. "A roofie? What the hell is going on? Are you gonna—what—kill me? Rape me? Torture me?"

"Yeah, all of the above," Shep laughed.

"In your dreams, Hook, in your dreams," Fricker said.

"And you," Jim pointed to Shep, simultaneously dropping the glass. But when the glass shattered on the floor, he didn't quite hear it, and he felt sick to his stomach.

Before he realized what was happening, Jim Hook felt the floor give out under him.

When he woke up, it seemed as if one hundred boys stood over him. They lifted him and took him somewhere very cold.

Chapter Twenty-five
Level Two

1

He felt a weird pain somewhere around his butt, like someone had stuck a needle in his left cheek—Christ, had they injected him with something? What kind of freaks were they? What the hell were they doing to him?

It was all sort of like a *Blair Witch* experience, mixed with a little of *The Ninth Gate* and *The Exorcist* as Jim vaguely saw—the words "through a glass darkly" came to mind—the faces above him, but not faces, the demons, that's what they were—no, they were skulls—no, they were dogs and cats?—what the hell were they? They kept shifting.

Oh, he figured it out. They were wearing Halloween masks. The cheap kind. Halloween was coming up in a couple of days. The dweebs. What were they trying to prove with cheesy masks? Shep Shepard was one of them. He was a geek. Fricker might be cool, but Shep was not what Jim would've guessed was Cadaver Society material. At least not with what he'd conjured in his mind, this secret nighttime group of unstoppable force and dastardly deed.

They might be losers for all he knew.

Yeah, losers who just gave you a drug which you swallowed like a moron and now you'll probably wake up dead, only you won't wake up, and instead you're gonna find yourself gangbanged or headbanged or banged in some disgusting and horrible way, or maybe they'll just do to you what they did to the senior last year—a bunch of underclassmen kidnapped and left this guy down at St. Cat's completely naked with profanities scrawled in magic marker all over his back, and fifty cents to call his Mommy.

That might just be a fate worse than death.

His vision went in and out of focus, and he felt a curious tugging along his shoulders and legs.

All right. They're carrying me. They're carrying me somewhere. They're going to do something really awful with me.

A few furtive whispers; rustling of leaves; someone groaned, and he was sure someone said, "Shit, he weighs a ton," and Jim wondered how the heck they had even moved him beyond the Trenches, for now, he saw the night sky above him, and the shadows of trees.

He looked mask to mask, trying to see their eyes, trying to see where Trey Fricker and Shep Shepard were in this group, but his eyesight sucked, and the drug they'd given him was making him feel nauseated.

Then he began to feel paranoid, and wanted to get away from them. Something was bothering him. Something in the back of his mind. As if an image had been burned there, and he could not quite remember what it was.

He looked around, but their shoulders and legs were in the way.

He glanced up to the sky again, but it was disappearing, and he was going down, down, down, down into some underworld.

And then wavering yellow light came up.

He knew where they had brought him.

It made his skin crawl.

It was the crypt.

2

They laid him down. He felt an icy floor beneath his back.

Christ, I'm naked. They stripped me. Oh shit, no, just my shirt. Christ, what is this?

Holy shit, what are they going to do?

Words began forming into a scream in his head and all that came up in his mind was:

Somebody help me!

3

"You have passed the first test, Hook. It was the test of trust. And you have restored it," Trey Fricker said.

"Yeah," someone grunted. Who the hell was it? Take off the masks, scaredy-cats. Jim giggled, imagining them all taking off their masks and beneath, a bunch of yowling cats.

"You sure did, Hook."

"You are now at level one. A seeker. Tonight, you must undergo a further proving ground before you become one of us."

"Before your initiation."

"To become an Adept in the Cadaver Society, you must pass the test of fear."

He was too sleepy and feeling too drunk and high and like he was floating up from the cold cold slab they'd put him on—he floated to the ceiling, he spun, he hung there awhile. A renewed anger washed over him, and he felt his blood rise. He wanted to beat the crap out of all of them. And then he felt a calm. The room began spinning.

Then, when he took a deep breath, he was just lying on the floor again.

"The test of fear is a test of your ability to

remain sane through a dark journey."

"The test of fear is to teach you courage and patience."

"The test of fear is to become one with the brotherhood of Cadavers."

"You have brought us the stolen ring, which symbolizes for us our core. That which was stolen by your brother has been returned by you, and redeemed your brother's memory."

"Your brother was one of our society, Hook."

"A sacred brotherhood which is based on the life of each individual brother coming together to stoke a great fire of brotherhood."

"We are a secret and powerful group, Hook."

"Tonight, you will sleep with the dead. You will remain here. You will not be able to move until morning."

"You will lie with the dead to prove yourself worthy," one said.

He recognized Fricker's voice as he felt a hand give his shoulder a squeeze. "It's all right, Hook. Remember, you need to conquer your own fear."

Jim felt himself being lifted and then brought down into some dark tunnel. No, it was like a lumpy bed.

No, it was . . .

And then he knew.

They had put him inside a tomb with a dead body.

He tried to open his mouth to scream, but it felt as if it were clamped shut.

He began to feel sleepy. The damn drug was having too good an effect, and he tried to fight it, but there was no fight in him—he was conscious of the feeling of something that lay beneath him, and he imagined a dusty skeleton crackling under his weight. He began to sink down, and he felt his throat tightening up, and then he was sure that whatever he slept with wrapped its arms around him.

4

But it was only the hands from above, the hands of the Cadaver Society, and they did something that terrified him even more.

There were trying to make him comfortable.

And then, what little light there was began to dim.

And he knew.

They were closing the lid of the tomb.

Chapter Twenty-six
Buried

1

He counted his breaths. They were slow and strained, and his first thoughts were like flights of wild birds—panicking winged thoughts of death and burial and terror and nightmare. Yet, nothing in his body raced. His heartbeat—which he could practically feel in his throat—seemed slow and methodical. He felt cold, but not so cold as to shiver. It was as if his body were turned off somewhere, but his mind was there, fighting to remain while the rest of him had deserted.

He could smell. That was the next thing he noticed. It wasn't an unpleasant stink. Almost like dried flowers. Chrysanthemums. Not rose. Not anything very pretty. Just a smell that was strong.

He tried not to think of what he lay beside and slightly on top of.

It was just a lumpy, hard mattress. He had to see it that way if he was going to get through the night.

Who knows?

They may pull me out of here in an hour or two. The Key Club had this hazing ritual where they made the pledges sit in a huge washbucket full of ice in nothing but their jockstraps. He had heard of a fraternity at Harvard that made its initiates jump naked into Boston Harbor in the middle of winter. Some of the guys had older brothers or sisters at Yale who told them about all kinds of bizarre and frightening rituals for joining clubs. This wasn't much different, was it?

Then the darkening thoughts came.

They were burying him alive.

They all thought it was a funny joke to stick the scholarship student in a tomb right before he gets kicked out for cheating. Serves him right. He was looking at another student's paper. In fact, Trey Fricker might say, he was looking at my paper, the creep, and he deserves everything he gets.

But what if they forgot him? What if they all went over and did their stupid secret society stuff and he was stuck here and no one came to get him in an hour? What if the air cut off and he slowly suffocated? What if something happened to them—what if they all forgot and then he screamed and no one heard him because the entire crypt was sealed? He imagined the days passing, and how he'd feel hunger and thirst and if the drug they'd given him—what was it, some kind of paralysis that he felt?—never wore off and he lay there until the last breath had left him and then someday someone would come down in that tomb, someday years later, and they'd find the two bodies lying together. His . . . and the bones beneath him.

Wait, you can scream. Surely you can. Open your mouth. Open it. Damn it.

He opened his mouth, but could not even feel his tongue or teeth and couldn't tell if his mouth had opened far.

And then he began to imagine things.

2

"Hey, Squirt," his brother said after the light came up. His brother sat on the edge of his bed, and wore a blue shirt and his boxers, the way he always did whenever he was just hanging out on a Saturday morning. "There's this girl I got to tell you about. I think she's something special."

"Yeah, I know," Jim mumbled, even though

he couldn't hear his own voice. "Ivy Martin."

"Yeah, that's right. She's something special. I didn't know you met her."

"Sure. I went down to New York and saw her. I saw her place, too."

"Did you see her paintings?"

"Yeah."

"She has neat stuff."

"You gave her some ring."

"You saw it?"

"Yeah."

"Where is it?" Stephen asked, his smile kind of twisting like he'd just sucked on a lemon.

"They wanted it. That's why I went there, I guess."

"They?"

"The Cadaver Society."

"Oh. Them," Stephen laughed. "Holy crap, Squirt, how'd you ever get mixed up with those geeks?"

"Yeah, I know. Stupid, huh?"

Stephen swiped his hand over Jim's hair, and then covered his eyes for a moment. "How do you know you're my brother?"

"I look like you."

"How you gonna make your big bro proud?"

"By doing the best I can," Jim said to the sweaty darkness of his brother's hand.

His brother brought his hand back, and Jim was lying in the tomb again, only there was this big light, and some shadow hovered over him.

Mischief

The shadow shimmered into a form, and it became clearer—Miles, the boy who had disappeared right before his eyes.

"Hi Hook."

"You're not real. You're a hallucination or something."

"Keep telling yourself that. You're in a tomb, right? With a dead woman all rotted and mangled under you. There are no ghosts, Hook. Just keep telling yourself that."

"You bet."

"Here's the thing: I'm dead, Hook. I've been dead for—well, a long, long time. And you brought me back."

"You're a dream."

"No, I'm something you woke up here, Hook. Something you started waking up a long time ago. Remember the night when your brother died? How you saw him? How he spoke to you and then something else was there, too? Something that you couldn't see, something up in the attic? Something's coming through, Hook, and guess what? It probably would've stayed in that little attic in your head except for one thing."

"What's that?"

"You're here. You're where we are."

"A grave?"

"Oh." The boy shivered as if an arctic breeze had just passed through him. "The world is a grave, Hook. This is Harrow."

"And what's Harrow?"

"It was built to bring back the dead," the boy said, and then the light went down and Jim was able to move. He pushed the lid of the tomb away, and it wasn't a tomb at all.

It was some kind of castle.

3

"Where is this?" he asked Miles, who stood before him wearing what Jim could only think of as a tunic, although the kid had some kind of trousers on, all wrapped up with shreds of cloth and rope, his feet bare.

"It's the place where I died," Miles replied, and then held his hand out. "Come, see?"

But then the sounds came up too—cries of children, the laughing of some man—the wet noises, too, as if something were being chopped open—

"He'll grind your bones to make his bread," someone whispered, only it wasn't Miles, and it wasn't his brother. It was *her*.

He saw her clearly, standing in an alcove of stone, and it reminded him of pictures he had seen of the Virgin Mary, or maybe it was Venus in some picture, but he knew who it was as soon as he saw that face:

It was Isis Claviger, the woman from the book he'd gotten from the school library. She stood there and smiled and then she began to fade into the stone wall.

But the man's laughter became louder, and Jim heard what sounded like a great hammer or club or axe slamming and scraping against walls, and someone cursing in—French? Was it French? It didn't sound quite like French, but it might've been—

The edges of the walls split open, like a wound, and blood began seeping from the stones, and Miles began shivering again, and whispered, "He took me to the Red Chamber. It's an awful place. The other boys were all dead. He made powders of their bones, and potions of their blood. The Red Chamber, filled with rotting flesh. And I was the last one. My name was Thousand, because he told me he had slain a thousand other boys before me in war and in peace. He told me I was a sacrifice to his god, whose name was blasphemy. He did terrible things to me in the Red Chamber before he killed me, Hook, he did unspeakable things, and then he took a great spike and opened up my stomach and poured my life into a large cauldron, and it wasn't just me, there were hundreds, and you, you resurrected me, you resurrected all of us, and worse, worst of all, more dreadful than anything in the world, Hook, but something's coming through, and he's coming through, he's coming back, and you brought him back with whatever is in your mind to bring him back with, and he's coming for you. You ripped something open and it's all coming through now and nothing can control it because you should never have come to this place. Don't go to the Red Chamber, Hook, don't let it out."

Miles's face rippled. The skin at his scalp began splitting down the middle of his face, and what looked like a spike made of brass shot up from his chest as if someone were behind him, jabbing him, and the spike tore down his belly, and a fountain of dark blood broke from the boy—

And something emerged from inside the skin as it fell.

Something's coming through.

Grind your bones to make his bread.

You ripped it open when you came here, Hook, you tore into it like a wild animal with something in your brain and you spilled its blood and now it's coming through and you can't control it and it's going to devour you and take everything you have because you are the key.

Wait for what will come.

4

Darkness seeped into his mind again, and he lay in the tomb and knew he was there, and not in some hellish castle, and then what felt like a large spider—

No, it was a hand—

Crawling across his shoulder—

It's an illusion. Hallucination. Dream. Anything but what he was afraid of now—

That the dead woman in the tomb—the skeleton beneath him—was reaching around to hold him.

This time, he found his voice, and he screamed at the top of his lungs, and felt sweat tingle along the back of his neck, and smelled the mold of the grave as the body beneath him filled with air and then began moving as he tried to escape the corpse's grasp.

And then he felt the ragged jaw against his neck, and the fleshless kiss.

5

Had anyone been in the crypt, he would've heard a bleating coming from beneath the slab of the sarcophagus, and the beating of arms and legs against the stone.

Someone might have heard the muffled sweet laughter of a woman, as if she had just found her one true love, and wondered if he were imagining things in the early hours of the morning.

PART THREE
INITIATION

Jack, a sack of gold stuffed into his shirt, the magic harp under his left arm, ran like the wind along the wall of the castle, but the Ogre was faster still, and when he'd caught Jack, he said, "You come to my table and steal my food and drink my ale and take all I have. Had you but never sought your fortune, you would not have met your doom. But you bring something to me that's as valuable as my ale and my food and my harp and my gold."

"What is that? I am a poor boy with no means," Jack said in reply.

"Your bones and your blood and your flesh," the Ogre said. "The beans you planted were not Magic, boy. You are the Magic."

Chapter Twenty-seven
What Will Come

Jim felt flesh growing along the bones that held him, and then he sensed others there with him, several bodies all embracing him, pressing their lips against his face and neck and lips and shoulders and scalp, and then he felt their moldering hands pressed into his mouth, and he could no longer even scream.

And the night seemed endless.

Chapter Twenty-eight
Dawn

1

Just before six A.M., six boys wearing plastic Halloween masks of skulls and goblins and ogres trooped down the warped steps. Each carried a candle or a flashlight, and they tracked their sleepiness with them as they pushed back the stone slab that covered the tomb.

Jim Hook lay there, his skin pale, soaked with sweat.

"You passed," Trey Fricker said, taking off his mask.

Jim looked up at his best friend and opened his mouth to speak, but his voice was gone.

287

"Who brought the coffee?" Fricker glanced over at the others.

A boy back by the stairs raised the Dunkin' Donuts cup in greeting, and took off his mask as he approached; it was Shep Shepard.

Fricker helped Jim sit up. "See? No skeleton."

Jim glanced behind him. Dried leaves and a few sticks had been his bed. There was no skeleton or rotting corpse beneath him.

Jim looked from Trey Fricker to his roommate, Mojo Meloni, as he drew the mask from his face. "Mornin,' Jimmy," Mojo said, passing him the coffee.

Jim's hands were shaking as he took the warm Styrofoam cup. He shivered and suddenly felt the iciness of the crypt as he hadn't all night long.

"Easy does it, Hook," Fricker said.

Jim glanced around the room. Mojo, Fricker, two upperclassmen, one named Wilson and the other named Peck, and then there was Andy LeCount, who was taking off a vampire mask.

None of their identities surprised him as much as he thought they should. They weren't some horrible secret society. They were guys who might as well have been outcasts.

Maybe Trey Fricker didn't fit the outcast mold, but he definitely wasn't what anyone would call pure Harrow. They all, in their own ways, didn't fit in, and the Cadaver Society might as well have been called the Guys Who

Tried Harder Some of Whom Were Slackers, Losers, and Maybe Just Messed Up.

"You made it," Fricker said. "You only have one last test."

Jim sipped the coffee and said nothing. It was nearly scalding, but he didn't mind. The heat felt good against the chills he was feeling. The drug, as it wore off, left him with a splitting headache.

He tried not to remember all he had seen in the night.

In the tomb.

Whispering to him.

After he'd finished most of the cup, they helped him out of the sarcophagus. His legs were wobbly. "You could've killed me in there," he finally managed to say.

Mojo passed him his shirt, which he put on. He went to a corner, and unzipped and peed; he didn't care that it was a crypt. It could use a little pee. He was surprised—and a little impressed—that he hadn't peed his pants all night long. It had been that kind of night.

"My ass hurts," Jim said. "You guys stick a pin in my butt?"

"We branded it. Slightly."

"Just a small C. Your left cheek. Barely noticeable."

"C for Cadaver Society. We did it last night after you passed out the first time. We iced your butt afterward. That way it doesn't really hurt,"

Andy LeCount said. "At least not for a while."

"Hurts now. Not sure I like people doing things to my butt without my permission," Jim said, and then he wanted to fall over laughing at what he'd just said. And the ridiculousness of it all. Even all his hallucinations. All the things he saw but could not have seen. And the pain. Not just where they'd stuck their hot poker. The truth was, every part of his body ached and seemed to sputter like a live wire. He was all nerves and twitches, and he wanted more than anything to just crawl into bed somewhere and never wake up again.

"Someone was always here to guard you," Fricker said.

"I don't believe you." Jim walked away from the group. At the steps up from the crypt, he turned and said, "Fuck you and your secret jack-off group. Fuck you for drugging me. Fuck you for your damn branding."

Then he turned and walked up the steps into the first rays of sunlight.

2

"Wait up," Trey Fricker called, but Jim kept walking, stepping around the grave markers. He still felt slightly dizzy, but did his best not to show it.

Don't look back. Don't deal. Don't let them get to you. Don't become part of this.

"Seriously," Fricker said, jogging over to him.

"I meant what I said." Jim kept his back to Trey Fricker.

"It's too late. You're in. All you have left is initiation."

"You lied about a lot of things. Like not knowing who the others were." He stomped over to the graveyard gate, drawing it open. The morning sun felt good, and his stomach was growling from hunger.

He had survived.

They could all go to hell.

"We're sworn not to tell anything," Fricker said.

Jim turned around, wanting to punch him. But he stood there, staring at him.

Fricker lit up a cig. "You'll know at your initiation."

"I won't be initiated."

"You will," Trey said, his voice too friendly. "Because you want to stay here."

"Look," Jim spat. "You don't know what went on here last night."

"Yeah I do. I was there. I was the guard. I sat and watched all night."

"Did you hear?"

"I heard you scratching and kicking and trying to shout. Your voice didn't work right, not on this stuff we gave you."

"This stuff," Jim laughed. "Christ, Fricker. I think it's called the date rape drug. Something

sociopaths give to girls so they can rape them.
And you know what? I feel like I got raped. I
wake up in the morning with a burn on my ass,
and my head practically cracking from a night
in Hell, and you bozos are standing around like
it's my birthday. You could kill someone with
that stuff. You could've killed me."

"You dead?"

"Maybe."

"Get off it," Trey said. "You want in and you
know it."

"I went through a lot of shit last night. I was
screaming. Things were crawling on me. I saw
things. I heard things. You don't even understand."

"It was all hallucinations, Hook. I was there.
I would've protected you. Honest," Trey said.
"We've all gone through it. All of us. No one has
ever not gotten out of there in the morning and
not been pissed off. Not one of us. I was pissed
off when I became an Adept."

"Adept?"

"This is an old society, Jimmy. My dad was in
it. And so," Fricker said, "was yours. And your
brother. You're a legacy. You're meant to be one
of us."

Jim laughed. He didn't believe him. The Cadaver Society was a bunch of liars. "And what
does it mean, Fricker? *One of us?* I get away
with cheating on a test?"

"No," Trey said. "You win. At everything you

do. We look out for each other. The 'Row's a rough place. The teachers are bitter and mean. Some of the students are shitheads who won't think twice about kicking you in the balls when you're knocked down. And it's hard to get through this place. The Cadaver Society makes sure you get through, and helps you out. It's a brotherhood. You get to keep your scholarship now, Hook, and you're going to find that you're a champion here as time goes on. All for one, and one for all."

3

Jim skipped his morning classes to sleep in, and by noontime the school nurse had come by to check on him. She was a husky woman with warm eyes and a faintly ironic tone in everything she said. "You have a slight fever, so I think you should stay in for the remainder of the day," she said, after taking his temperature. "I'm sure that's what you wanted to do all along."

"Mmm," was all Jim could manage before rolling back in to the peace and serenity of his pillow, where no corpses were embracing him into madness. His sleep was long and full of gentle darkness.

He awoke again at four in the afternoon. He took a long hot shower, and twisted around to look for the brand. Finally, he noticed the raised welt on his left butt cheek. It was so small as to be barely noticeable, but he got furious just knowing it was there. He also felt ashamed and somewhat used—that they had stripped him and branded him like he was nothing, like he had no say in it, like none of it was up to him.

When he shaved in the steamy bathroom mirror, he noticed that his eyes were bloodshot. He looked like hell.

He tried not to remember watching the boy as the spike had torn through his chest.

Or the feeling of a dead woman's mouth, pressed to the back of his neck as she held him.

Or another sense he had felt. The sense that Miles's words were right. The sense that there was something within him that had torn through life ever since Stephen had died. Something he couldn't control, and it was there in that crypt with him. It kissed the back of his neck and wrapped its arms around him.

It can't be real. You know that. It was some drug. It was your mind going wild.

Nothing is coming through.

Nothing.

But he had been there. He had felt those things around him. The dead. A woman had held him, her rotting flesh seeming to plump as she pressed herself against him. It hadn't been a drug. It had been real.

He broke out in a sweat, remembering. Trying to push that memory so hard back into some blank spot in his mind that a throbbing headache came on.

He set his razor down, and went back over to the shower. He turned the water on again, and turned it up as hot as it would go, and as powerful as the spray could get, and stood there letting it blast at his face.

Get it out of me. Wash it out. Please God clean it out of my mind. Get out the dead. Put them back in the ground or in heaven or hell or someplace other than here.

Even Stephen, don't make me see him. Don't make me remember when he came back to me, or when he told me things, don't make me remember his face and how even after he was dead I could see it.

I will undo every bad thing I've ever done. I will make sure that I don't get away with anything. I will not join some secret society. I will not run from all this shit. I want to make everybody proud, I want to make my mom smile again maybe just once, I want to have Stephen be proud of me, I want Dad to think I turned out okay, but I can't do it if it means remembering what got me in that tomb.

I want it gone.

Gone.

Even if it means my dreams go with it.

The shower began to cool, and eventually he had to turn the water off.

Chapter Twenty-nine
True Confessions

1

"No honor trial?" Jim sat in Trimalchio's office, his books on his lap. He had spent all the previous evening brooding in the library, brooding over his supper of meatloaf and potatoes, brooding in his dorm room, unwilling to talk to Mojo Meloni or anyone. He hadn't even called up Lark because he was afraid she'd think he was just messed up.

But now, Friday morning, the day of his Honor Trial, he knew his course.

And then this.

There would be no Honor Trial.

Just like that.

"That's right, Mr. Hook," the headmaster said, sitting across from him in a brown leather chair. "We have no witness now. We can't have a trial without an accuser."

"What about Carrington?"

"He ran away. His parents and the authorities are looking for him in Pennsylvania. They suspect he's gone to a friend's place. We found a note that stated his intentions. Apparently, he had some problems that were hidden from us here. But that's not your concern. You're off the hook, Hook." Trimalchio half smiled at his play on words.

"What about Mr. Kelleher?"

Trimalchio dismissed this with a wave of his hand. "He's not a witness. He did not see you cheat. Between you, me, and the wall, Mr. Hook, that's one teacher who has it out for you. I would not ordinarily tell you something like this, but one has to be realistic when dealing with schools. Mr. Kelleher," the headmaster said, his voice dropping to a whisper, "is a bit of a prig." He waited a moment to let this sink in. Jim wondered: had he said "prig" or "prick"? It was all the same to him.

Trimalchio continued. "But you'll get through the rest of the year if you just apply yourself a bit and perhaps don't let on that you dislike that teacher so much."

Jim grinned, but something within him prickled, and the grin faded. "I need to tell you something."

"Tell away."

Jim inhaled deeply, and held it. He felt that everything would change now.

There would be no going back.

"I cheated on that test," Jim said.

2

"Oh," Mr. Trimalchio said. "Jim. You don't need to say that."

"I didn't mean to cheat. I was scared that I'd lose my scholarship. Then I wouldn't be able to graduate from Harrow. It meant a lot to me then."

"And it doesn't now?"

"Not as much. Not after some stuff that's been happening."

"What's been happening? What would make a student confess to this? Not that I don't admire your honesty in coming forward, Hook. But what prompted this, when in fact you could be in the clear?"

"You told me about that poem. 'If.'"

Trimalchio nodded.

"I read it last night in the library. I read it over and over again."

"'If you can keep your head when all about you are losing theirs and blaming it on you.'"

"Yep. I thought about it, and it meant something to me, sir."

"And it meant that you needed to confess this."

"No," Jim said. "It meant that I needed to be who I am. And if I cheated on that test, knowing there was an honor code, knowing that I don't believe in cheating, it means something was going wrong with me and I wanted to be thrown out. Something doesn't fit right with me here. Cheating on that test was a cheap way of getting tossed."

"Well," Trimalchio said, leaning back in his chair. "Do you mind my pipe?"

"That's fine, sir."

The headmaster reached into his houndstooth jacket pocket and drew out a small dark pipe. He went through the ritual of loading it with tobacco and lighting it. He puffed on it in silence for a few moments. Then he said, "On the one hand, I'm pleased that you came to me with this, Hook. You have a great deal of insight into yourself, and I hardly ever see that with Harrow boys. Sure, there are some very smart and clever young men here. There are those who are blessed with looks and money and enough intelligence to go on to maneuver places like Harvard and Yale and MIT and Princeton. But there aren't many with that kind of self-understanding. I commend you. I'm impressed."

"Don't be, sir. I feel like a worm."

"I've found in life that low self-esteem seems to go hand in hand with teenagers who are brighter than average."

"If I were so bright, would I have cheated on a test?"

"Enough," Trimalchio said. Pipe smoke began to encircle his face. "What else has led you to this?"

"Sir?"

"This revelation. You've been looking like a ghost of your former self all week. When I saw you on Wednesday, you seemed happy and depressed at the same time. I would guess you've had four hours' sleep in the past three days. Something else is going on. Is it just conscience? I can tell."

"It's nothing."

Trimalchio sucked on his pipe and glanced over at the plaques and photographs on the wall. "I had a friend here, back when I was a student. My best friend, Hook."

"The one who killed himself?"

"Yes," the headmaster said. "We were so close, it changed me when he took his own life. He had violated the honor code, too. He was facing expulsion. I knew it. He knew it. But . . ."

Jim looked down at the floor, waiting for the headmaster to continue.

"Still, he killed himself. If I could go back in time, I'd change it. I'd erase all the years to get

301

back to him. And I'd tell him: All right, Jacky. You made a mistake. Make up for it. Do something so great with your life that you redeem your error. And I'd tell him something else, something I've learned in my own life and in watching the boys that come through this school. I'll tell it to you, Hook, since my friend is no longer here. Hook. Jim. It's not important whether you cheated on a test. What is important is that you faced it." Trimalchio nodded, as if this meant something beyond mere words.

Jim glanced up. He felt a brief confusion. "Yes, sir. But I still will be expelled."

"No, Mr. Hook." Trimalchio made a feeble attempt at a grin. "I think what has been said within this room remains within this room. Sanctum sanctorum."

"But—"

"No buts about it. You have had a moment of grace, James Hook. Accept it, and move on," the headmaster said. He stood up, wreath of smoke following him, and went to open the door to his office. "Now, on to class."

"You're one of them," Jim said in the doorway.

"Excuse me, Hook?" Trimalchio betrayed no knowledge on his face. Perhaps he was not a Cadaver. Perhaps he was. Perhaps it was all just screwy, this world of Harrow.

"Nothing," Jim said, and went to his locker to get his Geometry notebook.

And that's when he noticed the other book there in his locker, on top of piles of lined paper and textbooks he hadn't even cracked yet in Sophomore English. The one he had checked out of the library the day he'd been caught.

The Infinite Ones by Isis Claviger.

3

He began reading it during fourth period study hall, when he should've been doing his math assignment.

Jim found himself staring at the old photo of Isis Claviger, and found her less beautiful than he had at first thought. Some aspect about her bothered him, but he couldn't tell what it was. Then he checked the table of contents and saw words and phrases that seemed goofy, until he saw the one phrase that he should have noticed in the first place.

Chapter 14: The Haunting Rituals. Including psychic phenomena, poltergeist activity, telekinetic and telepathic waves, and Justin Gravesend's dream of a New Age at Harrow House.

Jim turned to the chapter and began reading.

4

I first heard about Gravesend's Experiment, as it was being called in Paris, when I was undergoing the spiritual vibrations at

the Malemort Abbey with the three Mages
from Rennes who had of late begun attract-
ing crowds and had set up a pilgrimage first
at Carnac, and then later at the abbey. It
was all but torn down, and the old men had
set up camp nearby. I had grown tired of
living in the wild to this extent, for it rained
three times a week and the cavelike arched
ceiling leaked tremendously. Soon after I
heard of Gravesend, he sought me out, as
is so often the case with the synchronous
aspect of Psi phenomena. I had, by that
time, gone to stay with James Witherel in
London for the British Spiritualist Society's series of lectures on astral projection.
Mrs. Cormorander had employed me to
contact her guardian angels, which proved
to be something I found impossible, although she paid me handsomely for sitting
at a table in her house for nine consecutive
evenings with no results to speak of.

Gravesend located me with a package
which included a first-class ticket for a
ship from Liverpool, and enough money
to make myself comfortable in the in-
terim. I used his generous donation to pay
off some debts I had accumulated, and
soon I was on a voyage to what became
the most intriguing and addictive study of
my career.

After several weeks, I came to the house in the Hudson Valley, and as soon as I saw what Justin Gravesend was planning, I knew that he was both mad with genius and the only man I would ever love.

He had created, with this house called Harrow, a museum of arcane and profane ritual, the side of human contact with the spiritual which rises above the merely passed-on and disembodied spirits of loved ones.

He intended to touch the Eternal with this house.

Although I had some fear at first, I felt it very much within the stones of Harrow House. I began to help him identify and find other artifacts and ancient texts in an effort to reach the Other Side. One of the easiest and earliest acquisitions to which I was party was the presumed bones and skull of the child killer, Gilles de Rais, as well as two of the instruments of his work.

5

By the time the bell rang for his next class, Jim had finished the chapter. He quickly flipped to the photographs in the book, particularly the one of a house.

Douglas Clegg

It was Harrow. It was different from what he knew, because the front of the house had been redone at some point since the photo was taken. The towers had been added, the entryway had changed. But the arches of the abbey in back, and the windows to the classrooms were the same, and the bit of land around it was similar enough.

He looked at the picture of Isis Claviger again.

There it was: Her hand held up delicately near her neck as she self-consciously touched her necklace.

The Alexandrite ring on the middle finger of her left hand.

6

After his last class, he went to the library to shelve books and help catalog some of the newer books that had come in that week. The librarian was busy in the stacks with one of the other students, pulling out books with bindings that needed repair. When he got a chance, Jim went to the computer and looked up the name Isis Claviger, but there were no books listed other than the one he already had. He looked up Justin Gravesend, and again, nothing.

And then, on a whim, he looked up Harrow

Academy, and came up with a pamphlet shelved under the Student Papers Collection called "Harrow Academy and Its History: A Senior Project by Jay Trimalchio."

Chapter Thirty
Friday Night

1

"You're telling me that Harrow is some kind of nightmare house?" Lark asked.

She had spinach between her teeth, which she must've sensed, because a moment later she reached up and scratched it away. They were sitting at the Lantern Restaurant in town, the cheapest place to eat outside one of the burger joints on the highway. Jenny had dropped Lark off at seven, and she had to roam the school searching for Jim, before she'd found him in the Great Hall entrance, sitting on a bench reading something that looked like a big book report in a plastic binder.

"It was called that, once," Jim said, excitedly, "according to what I read today. I'm telling you that there's something wrong here. Something bad."

Lark considered this a moment, and then dug her fork into a chunk of lasagna. "I'm worried about you, sweetie."

"Don't be," he said. Then, "I'm sorry. That was rude."

"Yeah, it was."

"Here's the thing. I haven't told you everything."

"I know," she said. "And you haven't asked about the puppy, either."

"How's the puppy?"

"Alanis is fine. Mrs. Burley said she'd keep her until we find out who the owner is."

"Good."

"Oh, Jim," Lark said, continuing to pick at her plate. "Tell me all of it."

"You can't make fun of me."

"I wouldn't do that," she said, and he could tell she meant it.

Then he began. He told her about getting caught cheating. He told her about the threat of the honor trial. He told her about who Ivy Martin was.

"Well, that's sort of good news," Lark said. "At least she loved your brother."

"And she was pregnant. But she lost the baby in the car crash."

"How awful. She was in the car, too?" Lark asked, her face registering dismay and sadness.

"No," Jim said. "She was in the other car. The one that crashed into them."

2

"She was furious, she told me, because my dad was trying to buy her off and get her to abort the baby. And Stephen was acting hurt, and not really sticking up for her. So she followed them out, intending to just follow them all the way to our house. And somewhere on an icy road, she said, she lost control of her car and it rammed them. She said she skidded along with them, and then her car spun and crashed into a tree. She was thrown from her car into the snow.

"But Dad and Stephen were dead.

"And her baby, too.

"I asked her about the story I had heard, about some farm truck, and she told me there *was* a truck, and it went off the road, but she didn't think it caused anything. She told me she would never forgive herself. But you know what? Stephen loved her, and that means something. Even now, with him gone. It means something to me. But she told me something else, too.

"She told me that Stephen had joined some kind of club, something he wouldn't talk about. She told me that he had begun to get distant even before the night of the accident. And that the club was bad, somehow."

3

"So, it's this secret fraternity you're involved with?"

Jim nodded.

They had finished up dinner—a bargain at eight bucks for the two of them with Special Lasagna Night, and were walking along the train tracks toward the depot. The slight wind felt good; he kept his arm around her as they walked, track by track.

"Why didn't you tell me any of this on Wednesday?"

"I just didn't know. I didn't know who to trust, really."

"Trust is hard, I know," she said, pulling away slightly, but taking his hand. Her hand was so warm it negated the autumn weather, the wind that swept the tops of the trees but calmed as it descended to the ground, the smell of river and leaves and distant chimneys—her hand kept him warm.

"You get this ring and bring it back to them, and they make you sleep in a coffin?" Lark had to work hard not to laugh. It did seem ridiculous to him, too. But he knew there was something serious in it. It was part of the mystery of coming to manhood, he knew. There were things guys wanted you to do to prove yourself worthy of their trust. He had known it in sixth grade soccer, and he had known it in wrestling, and he had known it whenever he had to make friends with a new group of boys.

It was some mysterious process of bonding, of creating a team where there had been none before. It was going to be difficult to explain it all to her. "In a tomb," he said. "They stuck me in one of those big stone ones. Down in the crypt inside that mausoleum up behind the school. They drugged me. They said it was a roofie."

They stepped off the tracks, into the streetlights along River Street, which eventually led back to campus.

Lark laughed out loud, and then saw he wasn't joking by the look on his face. The look on her face turned to concern. "Roofies? Rohypnol. People can die from that. Anything could've happened. Jesus, these are creeps you're hanging with. You should just tell the police. Or at the very least, the headmaster."

"I think he knows."

"What?"

"I think he's one of them. He wrote his senior project on Harrow, too. He knows about it."

"That people died here?"

"I don't think they died," Jim said solemnly. "I think they were sacrificed."

4

Less than an hour later, they were up by Hadrian's Wall, wandering among the ruins of stones.

"I haven't been entirely honest, either," Lark said. "I got two messages this week that are pretty disgusting. Whoever wrote them said you told them things about me. Maybe it was this group of Corpses."

"Cadavers."

"Yeah."

"What'd they say?"

"Just nasty sexual garbage. Dirty stuff, the way some twelve-year-old would to gross out a girl. It was pretty juvenile."

"Maybe it was them. Maybe it was something else." Jim put his arms around her, hugging her to his body, just to feel some human warmth.

She pulled away. "Jim, don't go off in that direction again, come on."

"I'm telling you," he said, feeling cold and lonely even there with her, "I was lying in that tomb, and I saw things. And something held me there."

"It was Rohypnol," Lark said, exasperated. "They gave you liquor and an extremely toxic sedative. It was probably like OD'ing on Valium or something, and you hallucinated. I knew a girl once who claimed some guy from some college in New England slipped one in her soda one time, and she barely managed to get away from him and three other guys before she passed out. It's an awful thing to do to someone. Criminal. Those boys are not friends of yours. Stay away from them."

"No, you don't understand," Jim said. "It's about my brother, too. It's about the night he died."

And then Jim told her about seeing his brother—flesh and blood—in his bedroom the night of the car wreck, and what he said.

And the thing behind the attic door, scratching to come out.

"Oh," was all Lark said afterward.

"That's it?"

"I don't know what to say," she added.

He watched her in the moonlit darkness. She was beautiful and distant even as they stood so close that they were nearly touching each other.

She didn't look him in the eye.

"You think something's wrong with me," he said wearily.

"I don't know what to think. It all sounds . . . fantastical or something. I don't believe in ghostly visitations or any spooky stuff, Jim. I just don't. Maybe you're overworked. Maybe it was that Rohypnol."

"Please," he said, reaching up to touch her face, his fingers stroking lightly her dark hair. "Believe."

315

5

"I need to go," she said, kissing him on the edge of his lips. He felt the distance growing between them as surely as if she were already a million miles away. "Jenny said ten-thirty, so we can get back by eleven. We both can't risk being out late again. If I miss her, I have to take the train back."

"Okay," he said, reaching for her hand.

She let him take it, but he felt ice. Still, he held her hand as they walked.

She doesn't love me, he thought. *It feels like it's over. She thinks there's something wrong with me. It's going to be over. Maybe not right now, maybe not next week, but sometime soon.*

As if reading his thoughts, she whispered, "You've had a rough week. So have I. All these midterms. All the crap you've gone through this week. It's understandable. Don't worry. As my dad always says, this too shall pass."

"Okay," he said, feeling only slightly better. "I'll wait for Jenny with you," he added, but too weakly.

"I left my jacket at the Trenches," Lark said, pulling her sweater down around the palms of her hands. "Can you get it for me? I want to just sit for a little bit." She sat down along the rim of the fountain. "And get me a Coke, too, okay?"

"Okay," he said, but he didn't want to leave her. He didn't want to break their connection.

He was afraid if he walked away, she would begin to doubt him, and then she would not want to wait for her jacket, and then she would be gone from his life.

6

Lark glanced up at the waving branches, and the sky, which was clear and starry.

Jenny began calling her name from somewhere down the drive, and she stood up and began walking toward the parking area beneath the shadows of the great trees to the right. But then, she distinctly heard Jenny again, this time calling from back near the school.

Lark looked up to the front steps, where Jenny sometimes would wait—although not usually on cold evenings like this.

"Hey, you! Lark!" Jenny called, and Lark glanced up.

Was that Jenny up at the window, in the tower? "How'd you get up there?" Lark giggled, and went over to get a closer look.

Lark put her hands on either side of her mouth. "You coming down soon?" she shouted.

Jenny didn't respond, and Lark wasn't sure if she saw her after all in that open window. But there was a light there, and she was positive that she had seen her. *Positive.*

She went to the door of the tower, and opened it.

Creepy. She stepped out of the bright lights of the driveway and entered the darkness.

It seemed to wrap about her like a cloak.

"Jenny?" she called again from inside. "You up there?"

ok to
record
male
real   11/04

Chapter Thirty-one
Initiation

1

Jim had just grabbed Lark's navy blue jacket from where she'd left it on the chair at the entrance to the Trenches, when he saw Jenny's boyfriend, Rich.

"Where's Jen?"

"She left fifteen minutes ago. Where's Lark? We were looking all over for you two."

"Oh shit, she's gonna have to take the train, then," Jim said, and ran back out into the night.

Douglas Clegg

2

He ended up running all the way to the train depot, but Lark wasn't among those waiting; finally, he returned to campus and looked around the fountain, hoping she had run to a bathroom somewhere and would be out there waiting.

He had missed her.

He clutched her jacket beneath his arm, and went back to the Trenches.

Lights Out had already taken place, and he knew that he'd be spending the rest of the weekend cleaning out toilets and wondering if he were cracking up, when someone pushed him from behind, and he landed on the floor, his chin hitting something so hard that he actually saw stars; he struggled against whoever had him, but he knew it was the Cadavers—they got a twisted cloth in his mouth, which they then drew back, and gagged him with it, tying it behind his head. Someone slipped a black cloth sack over his head. They ripped his shirt off, and someone tore at his shoes, and still another undid his belt buckle and tugged his jeans over his thighs and knees.

Fucking hazing! He cursed, but all that came from him were indistinct mumbles.

Then someone wrenched his arms back and tied his hands together, and then pulled his feet up behind him. They were hog-tying him, and it pissed him off. He struggled as hard as he

320

could, newborn fears bursting in his mind and a feeling that he had to survive at any cost, that he had to get away from the Cadaver Society.

They carried him out along the yard, and he knew where they would take him—up into the tower, up where Mojo had gone with him, had practically shown him the Cadavers' secret place.

Well, screw 'em. They're going to have to drag me up that long winding stone staircase if they want to get me up there.

He heard their muffled whispers, but couldn't make out anything of what they were saying.

The strip of cloth in his mouth tasted like sweat and made him gag, but he concentrated on breathing through his nose. He was going to get through this. Somehow, he would get through it. He couldn't see much of anything through the dark cloth, but occasionally, he saw shadows and light. They were carrying him up some stairway. Where to? The Great Room? One of the classrooms?

He saw more light and heard a door lock being rattled. Then he felt warmth, and they were now in well-lit rooms, and then he heard what sounded like the jingling of change.

Keys?

Old Man Chambers had been howling all week about his stolen keys. Master keys.

So, they had keys to something. But what?

He concentrated as best he could, but could

see nothing but shadowy movement, like moths fluttering.

And then he was being taken up a flight of stairs, but it wasn't curved like the tower stairs. It was—what? Another staircase? It wasn't the stairs that went up to the second floor classrooms, because they would've been making noise and echoing. He heard the grunts and groans of the guys as they pushed and pulled his body up the stairs, and every few seconds his knees and stomach grazed the hardness of the edge of a step.

Then, a landing.

Then, up another flight of stairs.

He felt like he was suffocating now, and his heart began to beat loud and fast. He tried to make as much noise as he could, but it sounded like a pig's snorts coming from him.

"Just relax," he thought he heard someone whisper.

Fricker? You asshole! You damn asshole for putting me through this just for something stupid that you probably helped set up in the first place! Screw you and your club! Screw all of you and your nastiness! When I get my chance, I'm going to kick your ass and everybody's in this club! I don't care if I'm a Cadaver or not, I'm not going to put up with this, and I won't put some other guy through this either!

Finally, after what seemed like hours but

might have only been ten minutes, they dumped him on a hard cold floor.

Then, he heard nothing.

It was pitch black, and he lay there on his side, still tied and gagged and feeling like it was a struggle just to get a breath into his body.

The sound of a door closing.

3

He lay there for a long time. How long, he wasn't sure. He thought he heard a fan whirring, but after a while he thought it was all in his mind. He stared at the blackness, unsure whether his eyes were open or shut. He wondered about Lark, and hoped that she had made it to the train, hoped that she wanted to break up with him after all. She was too good for him. He was basically, he knew, a cheater and a liar, and it didn't matter if he pretended that he didn't want to be in the Cadavers or not, the truth was, he had never felt he belonged anywhere, not since Stephen had died, and even the thought of his mother brought no comfort, because he knew that on some basic level, he was always failing her. The only shred of hope he could cling to was the idea that he'd make it through this ordeal—and the other ordeals that Harrow had to offer before he graduated, and then he'd get more scholarships, and he'd be the kind of guy who managed to get through it all, and eventually, he would prove to them that he was enough. That he could be one of them. That he wasn't just some poor scholarship kid whose family had once had some money but now had nothing, which might've been worse than just being poor to start with. If he'd been poor to start with, Stephen would never have gone to Harrow, his father would never have been there, either, and he could have just stood up for himself and not felt like every time he stood, they were on his shoulders, too, that he had to carry their memories with him to some future glory that life had taken from them.

You'll get through, Squirt, he told himself in Stephen's voice, and then it wasn't Stephen's voice, but Miles's, and Jim felt a wracking pain overcome his body. His muscles were beginning to cramp. The ropes that bound him hurt and he couldn't move other than to twist a bit in the pain of the charley horses in his calves, and the wrenching spasms in his back.

Eventually, he thought he fell asleep, but the darkness was all around him, so he was unaware of consciousness or unconsciousness. It was night where he lay. Someone was telling him something—

Every secret was meant to be told, and every door was meant to be open.

And he felt as if death were coming for him. He prayed a bit, which he hadn't done outside of Sunday Chapel in years. He prayed and then he cursed and then he thought he was dreaming and then he thought he could never dream again.

Finally, hours later, he began to convince himself that it was all right to be a Cadaver. It was all right to join up. He felt exhausted and weak.

Some kind of angel came down and brought a great light, and drew off the sack from his head, and cut the ropes from his ankles.

It was only one of them.

It was Mojo, in a purple robe with a hood. He looked vaguely ridiculous, but there was something haunting about him, too. As if he weren't just Mojo Meloni with headphones and schemes, he was something more with this robe and this candle. It was an act, surely. It was phony dress-up by guys who felt disenfranchised at a school like Harrow. Maybe guys who wanted more than just to get by or get through. Guys who believed that they really were running the show. Guys who were not the football quarterbacks or earmarked for automatic admission to the Ivys, but guys who aspired to things beyond sports and university. Guys, like Jim, who wanted depth to what they went through.

Guys who wanted to *believe* in things.

Mojo held a candle up.

Someone behind him—Wilson?—hoisted him up on his feet, steadying him. The aches in his shoulders and back and knees still roared through him, but it felt good to move, if only slightly. He was aware that he stood there in his socks and briefs, but he could not seem to feel the floor beneath him, nor did he feel cold or embarrassed.

Jim pleaded with his eyes, but was relieved just to breathe more clearly. His vision was blurred from tears.

"You have passed two of the tests of our Order, Adept. And now you will be reborn within the Cadaver Society. Tonight that which we call Mischief Night will begin. The gauntlet you must run is one of danger to both your body and your soul. We have been a secret and sacred society within Harrow Academy since the first year this hallowed institution began. Every Cadaver is connected to every other Cadaver in the brotherhood. We will protect and serve one another until the end of our days. No matter where you go, you will be a brother. Tonight, you will be inducted into the secret vows of our Order, and you will be initiated into the final test. The test of faith, the most important test of any of the Cadavers." Mojo had never spoken like this. How could he have been a stoner and a counterculture icon for so long and be part of something so strangely like a conspiracy? That's what it felt like.

They're not a group, they're conspirators, Jim thought.

Mischief

And I'm one of them.

Christ, I'm here. I have the brand. I went along with their tests. I didn't get away when I could've.

I'm part of this.

Mojo brought something out from his robe. It looked like some small gold coin.

"This is our symbol of eternal life, the ankh. It is an ancient mystery that represents for us the bridge between life and death and rebirth, for through our tests of trust, fear, and faith, you will have died, been buried, and resurrected again into life, newly born as a brother Cadaver."

Mojo took the ankh, which seemed a rusty brass in the candlelight, and pressed it beneath the gag in his mouth. Jim tasted the metal on his tongue. "You will hold your ankh in secret, forever, and you will protect it and never let another take it from you, for it is your life which is held within it. It is the coin of the realm from the passage to death and life, and in the ancient world, a cadaver had to have a coin on its tongue to pay the ferryman in order to reach the Underworld. This ankh is your coin. You must not lose it at any cost."

Wilson, behind him, said, "You will remain here for two more hours, Brother Hook. We will blindfold you, just as when we are born, we are blind to the ways of the world. And you will not move, just as when we die, we are locked within

327

our body. And you will wait in darkness for what will come."

And then Mojo blew his candle out, as did someone else in the room who Jim hadn't seen, and he stood there, the bitter taste of metal draining in his throat, his arms drawn behind him, his ankles tied together.

And all he could think was:

Please God don't leave me alone in the dark. Don't leave me alone in the dark.

I don't want to crack up and I don't want those things coming after me, those dead things, those visions of a seventh grader getting disemboweled or of the shadow of some man with a spike and a hatchet coming after me to grind my bones to make his bread.

4

Some part of him remembered what a psychiatrist had once said to him about imagining things, about a room with pads on the walls, and how he could put himself there if he wanted to, but if he wanted to live, he had to face things.

That's a Cadaver motto, too.

Face everything.

Those dildos.

Face everything. Test of trust, fear, and faith.

It was medieval.

It was like the Six Salient Points of the Holy Crusades.

It was like the damn Knights Templar with their secrets and rituals and hidden treasures and blasphemies.

Then, he began to think of Lark, and he felt better. Lark was probably back at St. Cat's, telling Jenny all about how she felt that maybe Jim was cracking up, but "I'm going to be there for him. He's having such a rough time this semester, but I just know he can do it." Jim imagined her faith in him like it was the sweetest thing he could dream up, and so an hour or two passed, and although he was beginning to see other things in the darkness, and although he tried to rest against something, every time he tried, someone pushed him away so he could only stand in the dark and think about Lark and how she would be with him and he would be with her.

And then, he was somewhere, some jumble of a room, walking through it. Boxes and old sleds piled in a corner, and lampshades torn, and a great steamer trunk; he stepped over and around them all, until he came to a short door. He tried the knob, but it was locked. He had to get out. He was someplace where he shouldn't be, and part of him knew it was a hallucination and part of him believed it was real.

And he pressed at the door, but it wouldn't give. He shouted at it, but his gag kept him from making more than what seemed to him to be the snarls of an animal—

Douglas Clegg

So he began kicking at it, and then scratching, and he thought he smelled a little boy on the other side, and he started saying, "Something's coming through! Jim! Beware! Something's coming through and it's almost here! You have to run! Something's coming through and it's something that you can let out, but you can't let it out, you can't let it out, Jimmy, because if you do then it will devour you and everyone you know and care about, and it's been waiting at Harrow for you, ever since it knew from your brother that you were born, your dead brother, it drank him up and spit him out, and they learned about you that night, Jimmy, how you could make them come out if you wanted to because you're the key to it, you're the thing that has this house awake, and you almost know it because ever since you've come here, they've been coming through, only they needed to push you to the edge, they needed to scramble your mind and fuck with your brain, and now they've done it and you can't control it, Jim, and you've woken this whole house up."

5

In the dark again. Hands tied. Gagged. Legs shackled with rope.

The bitter taste in his mouth.

That metal thing.

330

The ankh.

Glad he hadn't swallowed it. Just thinking of swallowing seemed to parch his throat. Then he began swallowing compulsively, over and over again. Can't swallow that ankh. Don't. You'll choke. Don't swallow it. You don't want to have that thing cutting through your throat and stomach and gut, poisoning you as it goes, and then out it comes again, cutting through your sphincter with its eternal life.

6

Sometime later, the light came up again in his prison room.

All six of the Cadavers were there, in purple robes and hoods, looking a little like demented choir boys. Each held a candle, and each held the small metal twist that he knew was an ankh.

"And now, the final ritual of your initiation," Trey Fricker said.

Two of the boys scooped him up by the arms, and he shuffled along, feeling every inch a prisoner about to meet his doom.

They took him into a room that was filled with a hundred candles. The yellow flames cast shimmering shadows along the walls.

In the center of the room, a body.

"This was a boy who died centuries ago," Fricker said. "Mummified through the years, he is the embodiment of the Cadaver Society, of life eternal, of the ankh which is our symbol."

"The ankh which is our symbol," the others repeated.

"You will partake of his body as the final test of faith with us, a faith which cannot be broken."

"Faith which cannot be broken," the others echoed.

They dragged him to the center of the room.

The body was small, and not wrapped as Jim thought a mummy would be. It was dried and shriveled, and to have imagined that it ever was a boy was well beyond him. It looked more like papier-mâché, and this gave Jim a glimmer of hope.

Of course they didn't have a real cadaver.

They were just guys like him, screwing up their lives in innocuous ways.

They untied his hands from behind his back. He tried to struggle against them, but he felt too weak.

Then they raised up the dried body, its eyes long sunken and dried into the gourd of its skull, and its teeth all but missing; the shriveled and tattered skin along its arms was ragged against the bone.

They wrapped the ropes around him, binding him to the skeletal remains.

"You will learn faith with this test, Brother Hook," Fricker said.

LeCount pulled off the gag.

Jim tried to talk, but he had forgotten about the ankh. He spat it out. It clanged on the floor. "Fricker, everybody, don't do this to me, there's something wrong with Harrow, there's something wrong with me, I won't make it through this, I'm making something happen here that I don't want to—"

One of the guys laid a hand on his shoulder. Another picked up the ankh.

Fricker squatted down in front of him and looked him in the eye. "Don't be afraid. Don't. It'll all be all right. It's just the last test. You've been pushed to the limit here, we know that. We had to rush this." Then he placed a new gag over his mouth—a long shred of purple cloth. "It's only until you experience the ritual." Fricker tapped the skull. "The original Cadaver Society found this little guy years ago," he whispered. "Apparently, he had been buried in one of the rooms. The guy who had owned the house had once collected mummies and relics and bones of saints. The first Cadavers found this guy. And he became a symbol for us. You will partake of him and then it's over, Hook. In the morning, it's over, and you're one of us, and you will be surprised at the changes that will happen. Once you're on the inside, once you're one with us, you will find you have brothers that you never imagined you had. We will leave your shirt and jeans and shoes here for you. When you emerge from that room in one hour, you will feel differently about all of this. LeCount here was your brother's Little Brother in the Cadavers."

Andy LeCount nodded, grinning. "I was in middle school when I joined five years ago. I was getting beat up regular by some of the juniors and practically failing math. Your brother— my Brother—tied me to the cadaver on my Mischief Night."

"It's a spiritual experience," Shepard added. "You'll see. It'll change you."

"Yeah," Mojo said. "There's something more to the 'Row than just books, Hook. There's something deeper. You'll feel it tonight."

"Now," Fricker said patiently. "Do you promise not to shout or scream, Hook?"

Jim nodded.

Fricker undid the gag again. "All right. Here." He went behind Jim and pressed the ankh into his hand. "Hold it. Don't let it go. It is your life and your light. No one can take it from you. You must not voluntarily give it up. It is your eternity."

"Something I have to tell you, Trey," Jim said, his voice hoarse. He felt a strange calm come over him. He was weary without being sleepy. He felt as if he'd been dragged through mud and brainwashed and spit out and still he was going to get through it.

He was going to get through it like Stephen had.

How you gonna make your big bro proud?
Trey Fricker leaned closer to him. "Yeah?"
"*Something's coming through,*" Jim whispered.

7

Tears soaked his face, and he felt a shivering go through him as they dragged him, tied to this creature, this dead boy, this skeleton, this pile of bones and rotted cloth—

And took him to a small door at the other side of the room.

"You will spend one hour in the Red Chamber together," Fricker said. "And then, when you return to us, you will be born again into our brotherhood."

8

The Red Chamber was not red but brown—brownstone—and just barely big enough to fit both him and the bones, which he now thought had just crackled as he pressed against them.

Four lit candles were situated in small alcove shelves slightly above his shoulders. He glanced around the small room—his head bumped the ceiling. But he saw a hint of shadows farther on. It wasn't a small room at all; it was more like a tunnel.

He looked at the skull with its emptiness and

then noticed that the rib cage of the boy had been broken as if by some force.

Who are you? How long have you been dead? Are you Miles? Is that who you are?

Am I going insane? he asked, although he was no longer sure if he opened his mouth or not.

One hour. That's all this is.

One hour in the Red Chamber.

With some ancient corpse.

I can do that.

I know I can.

The Red Chamber wasn't really a chamber. It was like a slim path between walls.

Someone had built a passage between rooms here.

A secret passage.

All secrets were meant to be told.

A way to get around Harrow without being noticed, he thought.

A way to hide things.

Things like this. He glanced at his new partner. His bosom buddy. *Ha!*

One hour, that's all.

You can take one hour, can't you, Hook? An hour with some old dust-farting mummy and then you can make it through this hellhole called Harrow and your mom won't spend her nights crying like she did after Stephen and Dad died, and you can be something more than just what you are, you can be better, you can make him proud.

And then the skull began to move slightly, as if with wind flowing through it. First to the left, and then to the right. The candlelight flickered and swept the shadows.

A wind? A wind in this airless place? This Red Chamber with its arcane ritual that reminded him too much of what he had been reading in Isis Claviger's book, *The Infinite Ones*, with its stories of ghosts and demons and how the man who built the original part of Harrow had a plan to imbue it with psychic phenomena, no matter the cost? How Claviger alluded to treasures plundered from every corner of the earth, the sacred and the profane, the blasphemous and the saintly, all in an effort to create something at Harrow that had never been matched in history. How silly it had seemed when he read it, the way that stories of devils and demons seemed silly in books on the occult, until one was sitting with a demon, tied to a corpse, in a small red room that was no room at all, but a narrow corridor between walls, a living burial, even if it only lasted for one hour.

And then, as he tried not to let it all get to him, the candles went out and he was plunged into total darkness.

"Fricker? Mojo? Guys?" he asked the small door, a door that had held just enough space to shove him through cramped up into this rat tunnel. Red Chamber. Rat Chamber. Rat Changer. Why did he think of Rat Changer? It was what they had done—the Cadaver Society. They had put him through sensory deprivation, hog-tied, and then standing there in the dark for the longest time—he had read about how brainwashing went in a spy book. He was their rat. They took away sensory input for a while to break you down. That's what they'd done. He was broken down.

Don't be afraid.

It's only the dark.

Please please, Jim, don't be afraid.

"Jim," Miles said to him in the dark, the dead boy's breath like sour vomit; he felt the boy's hands reach around his back. "You always had a way to bring me back. I've been waiting so long. All of us have. Lark's here, too, and we've been playing with someone who tried to hurt you. He was bad, but there are ways to keep him alive for as long as we need to until we've fed long enough."

"Why are you doing this?" Jim whispered, and he knew he had long ago crossed over into madness.

"You opened a door here, Jim. We've been

waiting all this time. A long, long time, for someone to come here and open the door and let us out."

"Who are you?"

"Many are buried within these walls," the boy said.

"Do they know you?"

"You still don't understand, Jim. It's all from you. You woke me up. You woke the others up. And now, we have you."

Small fingers grasped the ankh that Jim held in his left hand, and tugged it free.

The ropes fell from his hands and feet, and a green light came up in the tunnel. Jim began to see Miles more clearly, his face pale, his eye sockets bleeding and empty of his eyes, and his stomach torn open through the rags he wore. "We will never let you go now, Jim. We want you here always, with us. We've waited here within these walls for you, now you can come see your brother. Your real brother. He's been here waiting for you. The finger you found, with his class ring. That was a gift from us. That was what was torn from him the night he died. He wanted you to have it."

"I want him back," Jim said, almost involuntarily. "More than anything. I want Stephen back."

Chapter Thirty-two
The Door in the Wall

1

Jim crawled down the tunnel, skinning his knees as he went. He could still hear Miles's voice taunting him. Something animal within him moved him, even though his first reaction to the phantom had been to drool and feel as if he were going into that room in his mind, that hospital room from which there was no escape.

Don't be afraid. It's not real. It can't be. It may even be some kind of game.

But everything within him told him that Miles was as real as the ghost of his brother.

And the ghosts had seemed more real than the guys in the Cadaver Society. Were they part of it? *What in good goddamn is going on here*, he heard his father's voice say in his mind. *What kind of mess are you in now, Jimmy?* he could hear his dad say, almost over his shoulder and years ago.

The tunnel's ceiling rose, and the light was brighter. He found he could stand, and he began running down the narrowness, between the walls that seemed to move closer and closer together as he ran, until he came to the end of the passage.

An even narrower door stood there.

He pushed at it, but nothing happened.

And then, from behind him, he heard something moving.

Someone was thumping down the passage.

Toward him.

He felt his heart in his throat.

The footsteps were getting louder. Something was scraping on the wall.

Wait for what will come, a voice in his head said. Where had he seen that? On the wall of the crypt, written in blood, that first night.

Wait for what will come.

Where else? Somewhere else?

Then Jim remembered. It was the school motto:

Journey with Us into Enlightenment, and Wait for What Will Come.

Well, guess what? It's here. It's here and I'm here and I need some enlightenment, Harrow, I

*need to know what my place in this is and how
I can get out of this and I need to find Lark, I
need to see if they really have Lark, I need to get
her and I need to get out, please God, give me
some enlightenment, anybody, anything, any
ghost who wants to help me just give me some
enlightenment right now!*

And as he pressed himself against the door, it
gave, and as he fell backward into the room, he
scraped up his chest and arms, and he found
his balance as he slammed the door on whatever it was that was coming at him with that
spike that had opened up Miles once upon a
time, Miles and a thousand others, and Jim
turned into the round room he found himself
in.

It was a torture chamber.

2

Fricker set his cigarette down on the fat candle
at his feet. "It's been about an hour, right?"

"What's he saying in there?" Mojo asked.

"You said a shitload when it was your Mischief Night," LeCount said. "You went on and
on about how you didn't want to die."

Mojo cackled. "True, true. You bastids."

"Ten more minutes," Shep said, glancing at
his watch. He was half out of his robe, and
sweating up a storm.

"Let's call it an hour and drag his sorry ass

out of there so we can party before I fall asleep," Fricker said.

"No way. A full hour," Wilson said.

3

In the room that Jim Hook entered, there were racks and wheels and a mechanism that was once called a strappado, which dangled from the ceiling. Gas lamps lit the room.

"Here's the thing," Jim said to himself when he saw what was left of Hugh Carrington strung up on the wall, his arms wrapped in chains, shackles on his ankles and wrists, drawing them apart in a cross formation. "I know I'm insane now. I know it's like that."

Carrington's head swung slowly, side to side.

He had been opened up, and Jim couldn't even look at him, could not even look beyond the eyeless face of the guy who had accused him of cheating—accused him? Caught him! Caught him red-handed, and now they had done this. The ghosts. These ghosts were damn hungry, that was for sure. They wanted to play with them.

"You let 'em out yourself," Jim said, his eyes glancing at the weapons along the wall, the mace, the axe, the ancient battered swords. "You wanted to see your brother so bad when you were a kid, you became—what, a ghost magnet, ho-ho," he chuckled to himself, while part of him fought the fear and pain, knowing what the student he had never really liked must have gone through—Hugh Carrington, a runaway? Not bloody likely. Hugh Carrington had met up with whatever Jim had conjured here, some ghost of a kid who had been killed centuries ago in some castle by some Ogre. Hugh had just crossed paths with the Infinite Ones, as Isis Claviger would have said, Isis with her Alexandrite ankh ring, those damn eternal life ankhs with their symbols of good things like life everlasting, but they only delivered this . . . this . . . insanity.

"You're not really there, Hugh," he said. "Not really. It's my brain. I went crazy sometime this week, and you're part of it."

Miles materialized before him. "We tried to contact you other times since you got here, Jim Hook, but you didn't seem to see us. And what you've been going through this past week, it was a sudden thing. It was as if we finally got through." There was blood on Miles's lips.

"You're a dream," Jim said.

"I assure you, I am not." Miles laughed, spitting blood that sprayed across Jim's chest. "Ask Lark—" Miles motioned to what looked like a giant metal teakettle nearly as tall as Jim. "It's an iron maiden, very effective," Miles said.

"You told me you're French. And Miles isn't really your name. But you speak like anyone else. That means you're a hallucination," Jim nodded, and felt better. "I'm probably still in the Red Chamber with your corpse tied around my body, and this is part of it all. Mischief Night Initiation."

"I don't have all the answers," Miles said.

"And Lark's not in that iron maiden, is she?"

"See for yourself," Miles said.

Jim went over to the large metal container. It was locked shut. For a terrible moment, he thought he saw Lark's eyes staring out the rectangular opening at him, but when he looked again, it was empty.

"Where is she?" But when Jim turned around, it was morning, and he stood on the ledge of the tower window. "It's all a dream, isn't it? It's in my mind. It's like you. You're not really here."

Miles grinned, and then began laughing.

4

"What do you want more than anything else in the world?"

"You know. I already told you."

"Say it."

"You can't bring back the dead."

"There's a way to do it."

"It's a game," he said, mostly to himself. "It's only a game, right? Like a room in my mind. It *is* a game."

"If you say so. Believe what you want. No one

ever said you couldn't. But many have died for such games."

"It has to be," he said. "It's some kind of game. A test. Part of the initiation."

The wind brushed through his hair as he stood at the open window, looking down.

It was a hell of a long drop. He stood on the ledge at the top of the tower. He imagined dropping a water balloon and counting till ten before it hit the pavement. That's what it would be like. He'd drop and then it would all be over.

"Every game has its rules. I just need to know what the rules of this one are," he said, hoping the other boy would tell him something—anything—that would give away this game.

He kept feeling the tug of the earth—not gravity, but the need to be there, the need to leave the tower and return to the ground again. He couldn't keep from looking down.

The more he looked at the distance between where he stood and the earth below, the more interesting it became. It didn't seem like a fall, it seemed like he could just step over into it, as if . . . his eyes were playing tricks on him . . . but it was as if it weren't a long way down at all.

The other boy stood behind him and whispered, "It's just like a corridor, isn't it? You look down and see the drive and the stones and the fountain, but it changes when you watch it, the edge of your vision wraps around it, and it becomes a long corridor, and it makes you feel as if you could just step out into it, and walk that long way to its end, to find out what waits there for you. You can't go back because you know what waits for you there. You can't stay where you are. You must go forward."

"What's there?" he asked.

"What you want. More than anything."

"No," he said.

"Go on. You'll see. You can't stay on the ledge, can you? You can't go back. You know what's there. You can only go on. You want to, I can tell."

"What's there?" he repeated his previous question.

But the boy behind him didn't answer. He may have stepped away.

"It has to be a game," he said. "This can't be real. This can't be."

He stood alone at the top of the tower.

And then he stepped off the ledge.

5

And he didn't fall. He stood on air. It felt as if he could not fall, for the air was too solid.

He turned to see if Miles was still there.

The boy stood within the tower room, windows open.

"You can be one of us," Miles said. "We want

you with us, Jim. Your brother wants you with us."

"It's like magic," Jim whispered, feeling as if something else were close to them. When he looked down again to the driveway of the school, it was just a stone floor. He was still in the torture chamber. "It's just some game. I'm somehow making it seem more than a game, aren't I?"

But Miles's form began shimmering, and Jim rubbed his eyes.

It wasn't Miles at all, it was Stephen, his brother, standing before him.

"You don't understand, Squirt, do you? It wasn't you. You didn't bring me back that night. I wanted to see you. I brought myself to you. And I guess I brought something with me, too. I didn't know I had done it. But I had opened something in your mind, and it was like a key that needed to find another door. Harrow's just the wrong place for that." Stephen's image wavered like a candle flame. "I'll see you again someday, Squirt. Down the road. So many years from now, you probably won't know what hit you. Then I'll take your hand and we'll light out for the territories, just like Huck and Tom."

"Don't leave me," Jim said, feeling a bone-crunching pain inside himself. He wept, but barely noticed his own tears; he shivered but had no sense of warm or cold; he still remained fearful, but felt stronger for standing there, coming out of the fire. "Don't go. Please!"

"You can't keep me here. Even if you wanted to. I don't belong in this place, Jim. It's a bad place. It's unclean." Stephen's face darkened, and soon it melted away as if in an invisible rain, until there was just a shadowy ash.

"Stephen," Jim said, and his voice sounded like a baby's cry. If he hadn't been in pain, he would have laughed at himself. His brother had died years ago. This was a phantom. A reflection from his own mind. But he wanted the phantom. He wanted it so badly. He wanted to keep it there, even if it meant awful things happening, even if it meant things leaking out of Harrow, the others with their pranks and games and death—

He wanted Stephen to be there with him as he had never wanted anything else in the world. His mind ached, his flesh felt warm, and something deep within his gut churned and rose to his throat, like a shiver from his soul.

He wanted Stephen so badly.

So much.

He had to let the image and the thought go.

He had to, for his own sanity.

"Your sanity," someone whispered to him, "is mine."

And then he saw the small door open, and the others, his brothers, the Cadaver Society, there, waiting for him.

Only they wouldn't look at him.

"Holy Christ," Fricker gasped, drawing the two bodies, bound together, from the Red Chamber. *"Holy Christ."* He tore at the ropes binding Jim to the skeleton, the red marks all along his wrists and body, and Fricker pulled his friend against him and began weeping. *"Holy shit, no!"* And someone else—Mojo?—said, *"It's a joke, right?"* And still someone else said, *"Aw, fuck,"* and then Jim saw his body lying there, blood coming from his mouth and nose, a terrible grimace on his own face.

"Look at them," Miles whispered. "They only think about themselves."

"I'm not dead," Jim said. "I know I'm not."

"How do you know?"

"Because I know the difference now."

"The difference?"

"Between life and death," Jim said. "My brother told me I wouldn't die yet. I believe him."

"If you stay with us, you will never die," Miles said.

It had been an illusion, a trick, after all. Part of a game. The damned liked games, he was learning fast.

Hallucinations came easy to this place.

Unclean—his brother's word.

Jim was still in the torture room, and he knew

what to do now. He knew how to stop Miles and whatever else was there.

He knew the thing that scared even Miles: whoever or whatever had the spike and the axe, the monster who was buried somewhere here as well. Someone named Gilles de Rais? Was that the name from Claviger's book? A man who had murdered scores of children? Justin Gravesend had brought the bones to rest in these walls, as some kind of ritual.

You're in the stones, you told me so yourself. You're part of the house. I may have opened a door, but I can do one thing to close it.

"Something's coming through," Jim said, and the boy looked up at him.

"WHAT?" Miles screeched.

7

"Hour's up." Trey Fricker opened the low door, and peered inside. He was met with complete darkness. He glanced back at the others. "He must be shittin' bricks. The candles went out."

"LeCount!" Wilson slapped his forehead.

"Not my fault the candles went out. God, blame me for everything."

"Pass me one," Trey said, reaching his hand out as he squatted down. "Jim? You okay?" Mojo got him a lit candle, and Trey raised it into the Red Chamber, only the face he saw wasn't Jim Hook's, but that of a boy with dark hair, whose eyes had been gouged out, and the boy reached out and grabbed Trey Fricker and pulled him into the darkness.

8

All the other Cadaver Society brothers saw were Trey's legs shaking; but not a sound had come from his throat.

Then his legs settled on the floor, still.

Mojo went up to him and said, "Hey, quit clowning, Fricker," but when he pulled on Fricker's shoes, he fell backward. Fricker's legs came back, and the rest of him, too, only he was frothing at the mouth, and his eyes rolled up into the back of his head so only the whites were showing.

"Fricker?"

"He's joking, it's a joke," LeCount said. "Christ, look at him, it has to be a joke."

A small thin line of blood trickled from Trey Fricker's nose as he lay there, his body shivering. "Someone get a robe, something's wrong!" Mojo shouted. "He's in shock or something."

"Hook!" Shep said. "Christ, what's going on?" and then something emerged from the small doorway, and as it rose to its full height, they saw it was a thickset man with long stringy hair, wearing some costume that reminded Shep of a knight's mail and tunic—but all soaked in red—and in one hand he had a spike, and he said in a low voice, "Ah, my boys, so good of you to be here, I've heard so much about you from your friend Jim."

Someone—maybe Wilson—knocked over one of the candles, and his robe started burning, but he didn't even notice at first, and then, in the brief silence that followed, voices began whispering all around the boys, and the fire was tearing up Wilson's leg, but they saw the man with the spike, and even when the ripping began, and the fire tore through them, there were no screams.

9

"He's coming," Jim said. "Your friend. And others."

Miles began shivering. "Something's wrong."

"Where's Lark?"

"In the Red Chamber."

"What do you want?"

"You," Miles said.

"Dead?"

"Stay with us. You bring us back."

"No," Jim said.

"Either you stay, or she dies," Miles said, but something was terrifying him, although Jim couldn't tell what it was.

And then, he knew what to do.

Every secret was meant to be told. Every door was meant to be opened.

Every man was meant to die.

He closed his eyes, and when he opened them, he was in the passage between the walls, and it was dark, and he thought he smelled fire. He ran along the narrow path, feeling his way along the walls.

Finally, he nearly tripped over the small skeleton. He lifted it up. "Miles, you're not going to get to me."

He crouched in the doorway, but the room where the Cadavers had been had become an inferno. The flames licked the edges of the doorway.

The house was burning.

Then he heard a weak voice, and knew it was her.

10

His hands and feet felt icy cold, and a pounding in his head made him know he was alive, and possibly about to have the Mother of All Headaches.

He found Lark farther down in the darkness, crouched low, whimpering. "It's so dark," she muttered. "I . . . I got . . . I got lost. I thought I was in the tower and then I heard something. Some awful scraping. And all those things you told me scared me, and I started running and I tripped over things, and something was here, something was coming for me, and I . . ." She

355

coughed finally, and said, "How the hell can we get out of this place?"

11

He covered her as much as he could with his body, and took her out through the burning room. In the flames, he saw Trey Flicker and the others, standing in a circle, shimmering with fire.

He felt his body burning—along his back and his hair—as he pushed Lark onward, practically throwing her to the door. She was coughing, but she seemed all right. It would be all right, he knew. If he could just get her out of all this.

He pressed the door to get out, but it wouldn't budge.

"Open it, Miles," he whispered. "Open it. You promised. I will give you what you want!"

The flames licked at the edges of his consciousness. He had to get through them, he had to get Lark out, away from the ghosts and the fire.

"You promised, Miles!" he shouted. "Every door is meant to be opened! You promised me!"

Epilogue

November was bitter cold, and he spent every day at her bedside in the hospital. School was an impossibility, ever since the media had descended upon Watch Point, with stories of the dead students, the haunting, the things found in parts of Harrow, and the tales from the locals about ghosts and devils on Halloween. Harrow Academy had all but burned to the ground. Half the country thought Watch Point was the biggest tragedy of school violence in history; others felt what had happened at that school was a sign of the times.

But Jim didn't notice most of this; he just noticed Lark, and how she lay in a coma, her burns healing, but didn't seem to respond to

Douglas Clegg

anything or anyone. Her parents had come, but
were advised that she should not be moved for
the time being; they hired a nurse to sit with
her when they couldn't be there; but Jim was
there most days and nights, and sometimes
slept on the floor.

Finally, in early December, she opened her
eyes, and by Christmas, she was drinking liq-
uids and able to say something.

"Jim," she whispered as he clutched her
hand. "Jim. I saw . . . all of them."

He nodded. "I know."

"Harrow—" she began, but stopped. She
needed some water. He got her a cup of ice, and
she put a sliver in her mouth, sucking on it. "It
was an awful place."

"Yeah."

"Jim, what is it about, what we saw there?
Was it real? Were those really . . ."

He leaned forward and put his hand over
hers. "It's like what I've been thinking." He
wanted to continue and say, *we never know if
what we go through in life is what's really in front
of us or if it's just shadows of something else.
Some greater scheme*. But looking at her, all that
she meant to him, and all that she meant
whether or not he was there, what Lark meant
to the world, was more precious to him right
then than any words could express.

And then he leaned down and pressed his
cheek lightly against her palm. "I don't care

about that, Lark. All I care about is you're getting better."

He watched himself say this, all of this, as if it were a dream.

He was there with her, and they were making plans about going back to school after Christmas, about seeing each other for New Year's Eve, and Lark said, "Be here with me, Jim. That's all I want. Be here with me."

"Always," he whispered, and then he felt it take him over, and he knew he had to return to the Red Chamber, return again and again, because he was now part of Harrow.

But it had been worth it. At least Lark was safe.

DOUGLAS

HALLOWEEN

THE

MAN

CLEGG

The New England coastal town of Stonehaven has a history of nightmares—and dark secrets. When Stony Crawford becomes a pawn in a game of horror and darkness, he finds that he alone holds the key to the mystery of Stonehaven, and to the power of the unspeakable creature trapped within a summer mansion.

___4439-0 $6.99 US/$8.99 CAN

Dorchester Publishing Co., Inc.
P.O. Box 6640
Wayne, PA 19087-8640

NIGHTMARE CHRONICLES

DOUGLAS CLEGG

It begins in an old tenement with a horrifying crime. It continues after midnight, when a young boy, held captive in a basement, is filled with unearthly visions of fantastic and frightening worlds. How could his kidnappers know that the ransom would be their own souls? For as the hours pass, the boy's nightmares invade his captors like parasites—and soon, they become real. Thirteen nightmares unfold: A young man searches for his dead wife among the crumbling buildings of Manhattan… A journalist seeks the ultimate evil in a plague-ridden outpost of India… Ancient rituals begin anew with the mystery of a teenage girl's disappearance… In a hospital for the criminally insane, there is only one doorway to salvation… But the night is not yet over, and the real nightmare has just begun. Thirteen chilling tales of terror from one of the masters of the horror story.

___4580-X $6.99 US/$8.99 CAN

YOU COME WHEN I CALL YOU

DOUGLAS CLEGG

An epic tale of horror, spanning twenty years in the lives of four friends—witnesses to unearthly terror. The high desert town of Palmetto, California, has turned toxic after twenty years of nightmares. In Los Angeles, a woman is tormented by visions from a chilling past, and a man steps into a house of torture. On the steps of a church, a young woman has been sacrificed in a ritual of darkness. In New York, a cab driver dreams of demons while awake. And a man who calls himself the Desolation Angel has returned to draw his old friends back to their hometown—a town where, two decades earlier, three boys committed the most brutal of rituals, an act of such intense savagery that it has ripped apart their minds. And where, in a cavern in a place called No Man's Land, something has been waiting a long time for those who stole something more precious than life itself.

___4695-4 $7.99 US/$9.99 CAN

DOUGLAS CLEGG
THE ATTRACTION

The signs all along the desert highway read "Come See the Mystery!" But some mysteries should remain buried forever. Like the mummified remains of an ancient legendary flesh-scraper, whose job had been to scrape the flesh off the bones of human sacrifices…

When a car filled with teenagers gets a flat tire, the kids figure they have time to check out the Mystery. Behind curtains lies a small, withered corpse with very long fingernails. Above it, tacked on the wall, is a sign: "Do Not Touch. Do Not Feed." But it has to be a hoax, right? How could anyone know that the flesh-scraper is hungry for flesh?

Dorchester Publishing Co., Inc.
P.O. Box 6640
____5411-6
Wayne, PA 19087-8640
$6.99 US/$8.99 CAN

DOUGLAS CLEGG
THE ABANDONED

There is a dark and isolated mansion, boarded-up and avoided, on a hill just beyond the town of Watch Point in New York's Hudson Valley. It has been abandoned too long and fallen into disrepair. It is called Harrow and it does not like to be ignored. But a new caretaker has come to Harrow. He is fixing up the rooms and preparing the house for visitors....

What's been trapped inside the house has begun leaking like a poison into the village itself. A teenage girl sleeps too much, but when she awakens her nightmares will break loose. A little boy faces the ultimate fear when the house calls to him. A young woman must face the terror in her past to keep Harrow from destroying everything she loves. And somewhere within the house a demented child waits with teeth like knives.

PANDORA DRIVE

TIM WAGGONER

The small town of Zephyr, Ohio, is home to a very special young woman. Damara is reclusive—and she has the ability to make other people's dreams, fears and fantasies all too real. But this isn't an ability that she can control, as many people in town are beginning to learn. For some, dreams are becoming living nightmares. For others, their deepest fears are suddenly alive and worse than they ever imagined.

As Damara's powers sweep like a wildfire through the town, her neighbors' long-hidden desires are dragged out into the open—and given life. But as the old saying goes, be careful what you wish for, because in this case...it could kill you.

DEATHBRINGER

BRYAN SMITH

Hannah Starke was the first to die. And the first to come back. In the small town of Dandridge they all come back. The buried claw their way out of their graves. The recently killed get up and kill. As the dead attack the living, the numbers of the dead continue to grow. And the odds against the living get worse and worse.

In the middle of it all stands a dark, shadowy figure, a stranger in town with an unspeakable goal. If he is successful, death will rule Dandridge and the terror will continue to spread until all hope is lost. Who can defeat an army of the living dead? Who can stand face-to-face against the...

DEATHBRINGER

BERSERK

TIM LEBBON

"They kept monsters." That's what Tom overhears in the bar. And he hears more things that can finally lead him to the truth about his son's death ten years before. The army had said it was a training accident. But why had the coffin they sent home been sealed?

So on a dark night, in a deserted field, Tom begins to unearth the mass grave where he hopes—and fears—that he will find his son's remains. He finds instead madness: corpses in chains and dead bodies that still move and grasp and clutch. And one little girl, dead and rotting, who promises to help Tom find what he's looking for, if only he will free her...

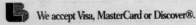